Magical Prepositional Phrasal Verbs

圖解介系詞
看故事學片語

第一本文法魔法書！

結合**圖解**和**故事**搞懂英文介系詞
和片語的**MAGICAL**學習法!!!

特色【圖解介系詞篇】 圖解中的主角魔法兔帶你一步步，依循魔法箭頭指標，搭配關鍵例句，介系詞的概念漸漸浮現於腦海中，瞬間了解表達物體去向（to、from）、物體所在（in、on、at）等20大介系詞！

特色【看故事學片語篇】 閱讀故事人物【Ep. 1-2愛戀】與【Ep. 3工作】過程、【Ep. 4孩童】的時光**4**大情境，片語從展讀故事時，同步學習、吸收。

趙婉君◎著

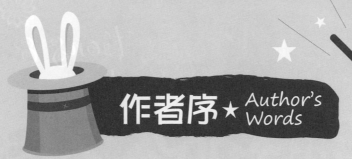

作者序 ★ Author's Words

　　當英語學習融入生活中時，英語是一個溝通工具，這時學英文就像週末的下午，你想拿起一本短篇故事，小讀一番這麼簡單，你會發現用英文你也可以感受別人眼中的世界，並為自己的世界增添一些情趣。

　　你可以把這本《圖解介系詞、看故事學片語：第一本文法魔法書》當作故事來讀，從中你會看到人物於戀愛時的一見鍾情、相處上的摩擦與掙扎；在工作中的迷惘與追尋，以及孤兒院孩子的童言童語，這時Fiona老師會在每個劇情的轉折處，帶著你從情境切入文法重點學英文。本書主要能培養你的片語詞彙、片語的組成（通常為動詞＋介系詞）概念；片語也是**某個動詞**與其**習慣搭配介系詞**的合體。本書的特色在於能讓你透過「圖解」了解介系詞的空間意涵，以及其延伸到生活中的應用，從此不再死記介系詞和片語！

趙婉君

編者序 ★ Editor's Words

　　本書結合【圖解】和【故事】獨特的學習方式，就是希望能幫助讀者搞懂英文介系詞的概念，以及片語如何活用。

　　其中 Part 1【圖解介系詞篇】有魔法兔插圖標示出【介系詞】的用法，並搭配例句，介系詞基礎概念一目了然。而 Part 2【看故事學片語篇】則帶著讀者一邊體會故事人物【Ep.1-2 愛戀中】的心情轉折、【Ep. 3 工作時】的拼勁，也從【Ep.4 孩童的角度】看世界，並在懵懂中成長的 4 大情境學片語，強化對片語的概念！

　　兩大篇章都有精心規劃的小單元，在 Part 1【圖解介系詞篇】每單元後放入「動詞和介系詞配對」、「介系詞小學堂」小單元，讀者能在這裡看清介系詞的多元面向，同時立即驗收學習效果！

　　於 Part 2【看故事學片語篇】的每單元後，則有「片語有道理」、「一字多義」小單元，並透過這些小單元整理出同類型的片語，目的都在加速學習者對片語的理解，擴增片語量！

　　現在就一同體驗魔法文法書的魅力，讓英文「讀」、「寫」、「說」的能力突飛猛進吧！

編輯部

使用說明

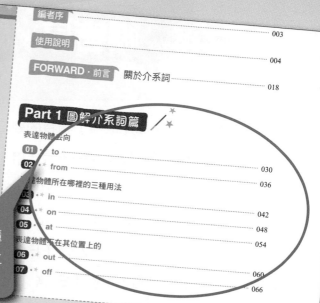

1 目次分類詳細，一有不懂的介系詞，查找一翻就到，立即解決問題！

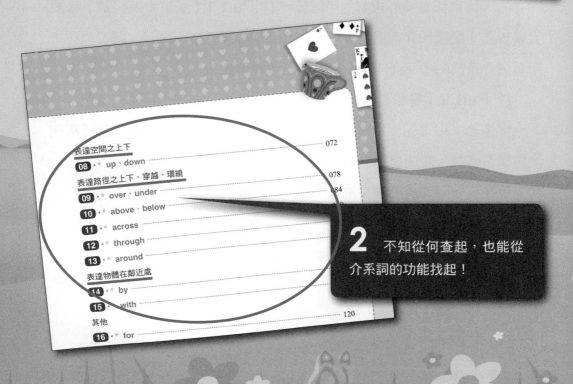

2 不知從何查起，也能從介系詞的功能找起！

2 「不知從何查起，也能從介系詞的功能找起！」

3 翻一翻有趣的情境愛情、友情與工作故事，邊看故事，邊學片語！

Part 2 看故事學片語篇

Episode 1: Meeting the One and Only 遇見真命天子

關於介系詞

介系詞基礎問答

Q1：介系詞是什麼？

ans 介系詞，用來表達「物體間的空間關係」，例如：椅子、桌間等實質的東西；也可以表達抽象的事物。人類透過想像力，將空間的概念比喻到事物上，與抽象的事物（時間）以及情感（好心情）做連結，因此引申出很多意涵。

♠ 以抽象的時間來說：
There is a press conference on Tuesday.
（星期二有一場記者會。）

♠ 以抽象的情緒來說：
When the situation presented itself, I felt the mood of everyone in the room became down.
（當事情浮出檯面，我感覺房內大家的心情都變差了。）

18

Q2：介系詞怎麼學？

ans 介系詞很常見，出現時卻又不是你理解的那個意思。你可能會想，介系詞到底有沒有規律可循？介系詞其實難在它的一字多義，而當你先知道基礎的「空間意涵」，再來了解「引申意涵」，接著進而用片語的模式來理解「與介系詞一同出現的搭配詞」，相信你一定會對介系詞有更近一步的了解。

♠ 重點 1：從「語意」來習得
本書將會一一介紹常見、實用的介系詞，並從中……
(1) 了解介系詞的空間意涵（spatial meaning）。
(2) 了解介系詞從空間引申的語意（metaphorical meaning）或其他……

♠ 重點：從「介系詞的搭配」來記憶與理解
……連用的介系詞：「動詞＋介系詞」
……ou can count on me.
……你可以依靠我。）
……ver lie to yourself.
……不要對自己說謊。）
……light departs from Terminal 1.
……那班飛機從第一航廈起飛。）

19

---

4 先看介系詞常見 Q&A 問答，循序漸進了解介系詞！

♠ 談到空間關係時，to 表達「物體間方向性」，中文意思為「從……去……」的意思。from「從……來……」為其相反詞。

關鍵例句
Mary walks to the kitchen and opens the refrigerator.
（瑪莉走到廚房並打開冰箱。）

解析
「動作＋ to ＋地點」表示了動作的路徑與終點。

30

5 看圖搭配關鍵例句，看懂介系詞怎麼用！

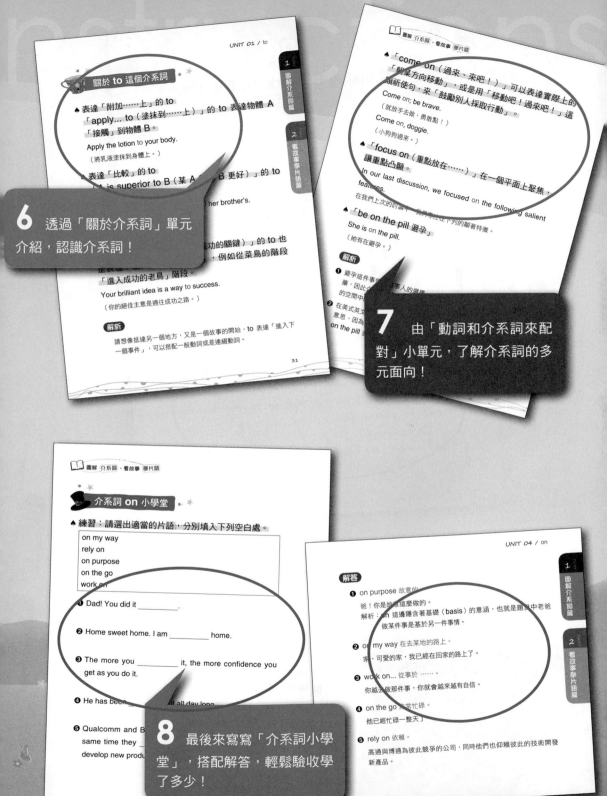

關於 **to** 這個介系詞

◆ 表達「附加……上」的 to
「apply... to（塗抹到……上）」的 to 表達物體 A
「接觸」到物體 B。

Apply the lotion to your body.
（將乳液塗抹到身體上。）

◆ 表達「比較」的 to
「A is superior to B（某 A 比 B 更好）」的 to
⋯⋯ her brother's.

⋯⋯成功的關鍵）」的 to 也
⋯⋯，例如從菜鳥的階段

「進入成功的老鳥」階段。

Your brilliant idea is a way to success.
（你的絕佳主意是通往成功之路。）

解析
請想像抵達另一個地方，又是一個故事的開始，to 表達「進入下
一個事件」，可以搭配一般動詞或是連綴動詞。

31

6 透過「關於介系詞」單元
介紹，認識介系詞！

圖解 **介系詞**‧看故事 **學片語**

◆「come on（過來、來吧！）」可以表達實際上的
「朝某方向移動」，或是用「移動吧！過來吧！」這
種祈使句，來「鼓勵別人採取行動」。

Come on; be brave.
（就放手去做，勇敢點！）
Come on, doggie.
（小狗狗過來。）

◆「focus on（重點放在……）」在一個平面上聚焦，
讓重點凸顯。

In our last discussion, we focused on the following salient
features.
（在我們上次的討論，我們聚焦在下列的顯著特徵。）

◆「be on the pill 避孕」
She is on the pill.
（她有在避孕。）

解析
❶ 避孕這件事⋯⋯⋯⋯平人的選達
藥，因此在⋯⋯⋯⋯
的空間中⋯⋯⋯

❷ 在美式英文⋯⋯
意思，因為⋯⋯
on the pill ⋯⋯

7 由「動詞和介系詞來配
對」小單元，了解介系詞的多
元面向！

圖解 **介系詞**‧看故事 **學片語**

介系詞 **on** 小學堂

◆ 練習：請選出適當的片語，分別填入下列空白處。

| on my way |
| rely on |
| on purpose |
| on the go |
| work on |

❶ Dad! You did it _____.

❷ Home sweet home. I am _____ home.

❸ The more you _____ it, the more confidence you
get as you do it.

❹ He has bee⋯⋯⋯⋯ all day long.

❺ Qualcomm and B⋯⋯
same time they ⋯⋯
develop new produ⋯⋯

52

8 最後來寫寫「介系詞小學
堂」，搭配解答，輕鬆驗收學
了多少！

解答

❶ on purpose 故意的
爸！你是故意這麼做的。
解析：on 這邊隱含著基礎（basis）的意涵，也就是題目中老爸
做某件事是基於另一件事情。

❷ on my way 在去某地的路上。
家，可愛的家，我已經在回家的路上了。

❸ work on... 從事於 ……。
你越去做那件事，你就會越來越有自信。

❹ on the go 非常忙碌
他已經忙碌一整天。

❺ rely on 依賴
高通與博通是彼此競爭的公司，同時他們也仰賴彼此的技術開發
新產品。

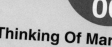

unit 06

Thinking Of Mark All The Time
魂不守舍

 片語搶先看

1. look at 看著	2. watch ones' step 小心
3. fall to the ground 跌倒	4. in time 在某截止時間之內／及時
's aid 前來	6. no big deal 沒事的、不麻煩

9 從「片語搶先看」，快速抓住每單元重點片語

看對話學英文

Barbara and her boss, Mr. Cooper, made an appointment with Eve to come to the factory for the evaluation. Eva waits for their coming in front of the building. At the end of the street comes a white convertible. The car stops right at the factory;a tall man comes out of it. Eva looked at him with astonishment.

芭芭拉和他的老闆庫伯先生和伊娃約好時間到工廠來做評估。伊娃在工

Only / 遇見真命天子
The Time / 魂不守舍

廠前面等待他們的到來，街尾出現了一台白色敞篷車，就停在工廠前，一位高大的男子走出來，伊娃看震驚地看著他。

E ▶ Eva 伊娃　　**B** ▶ Barbara 芭芭拉　　**C** ▶ Mr. Cooper 庫柏先生

B This is Mr. Cooper. This is Miss Griffin, the real estate agent representing the owner of the property.

（這位是庫伯先生，這位是格里芬小姐，她是房地產經紀人，代表這間工廠的老闆出售資產。）

E Mark?

（馬可？）

B Do you know each other?

（你們認識彼此嗎？）

Mr. Cooper ignores his secretary's question.

庫伯先生忽略了他秘書的問題。

C It's nice meeting you, Miss Griffin.

（很高興認識你，格里芬小姐。）

They walk into the factory for a tour.

9 看「對話」讀故事，學片語。有情境，更好學！

1 圖解介系詞篇

2 看故事學片語篇

看日記學英文

To avoid the annoying heat from the sun, Mark and I ended up having the dinner at a self-serve ice cream shop. We arrived at the shop around noon, and it is full of people. People all lined up for ice cream machines, so we had to wait for a while. Aside from the long wait, it was fun to learn about him based on his topping choices. He gave himself a nick name of Mr. Gummy Bear. At the same time, I was called the Healthy

10 還有從「日記」看故事，學片語；每片語皆有套色，重點片語一目了然！

Ep 1 : Meeting the One and Only / 遇見真命天子
Unit 7 He Is Really Into Me. / 他真的很愛我

片語有道理

不管是在戀愛中還是各種人際關係的相處，兩個人以上的相處都會遇到要決定事情的時候，若意見不合，則需要一方妥協或讓步，表示妥協的英文片語有：

give in 投降，表示完全讓步。

Thomas is very stubborn. He doesn't know the meaning of giving in, and he never makes compromises.

（湯馬士非常固執，他不知道投降是什麼，也從不退讓。）

make compromises 妥協，表示部分讓步。

Thomas believes that ... kind of girl who makes comp...

（湯馬士相信他的... 女人。）

meet somebod...

Jamie tries to make ...

（潔咪試著要讓湯馬士對她讓步，但總是失敗。）

註 compromise 這個字是由 com＋promise 所組成的，com 這個字

11 片語篇特收錄「片語有道理」與「一字多義」單元，全面了解片語的用法！

Ep 2 : Getting Close Or Distant / 越來越好，還是漸行漸遠？
Unit 8 Eva Moves In Mark's Apartment. / 同居了

一字多義

♠ **move in** 搬家、**step in** 出手幫忙、**jump in** 插話

move（移動）、step（踏步）、jump（跳躍）都是指身體的動作，但都搭配介係詞 in（進入......），意思就不只是身體的動作那麼單純了：

• **move** 變換身體的姿勢、移動。**move in** 搬進新居，英文意思為 To begin living in a new place。

A celebrity moves in the community last month.
（一位名流上個月搬進了這個社區。）

step 將腳抬起、踏步。**step in** 介入，出手幫忙，英文意思為 to become involved in a difficult situation in order to offer help。

When do the social workers think it's time to step in for stray ...gs?

（...工人員什麼時候覺得是時候該出手解決流浪狗的問題呢？）

...利用腿跟腳快速離開地面、跳躍。**jump in** 插話，...插入跟原本對話無關的主題，英文意思為 To ...pt others' conversation.

...ve to jump in here.
（...必須在這邊打斷一下。）

CONTENTS

Part 2 看故事學片語篇

Episode 2: Growing Close or Distant
越來越好，還是漸行漸遠？

Episode 3: A Job, a Career, or a Calling
一份工作、一份職業、還是一個志業？

關於介系詞

 介系詞基礎問答

Q1：介系詞是什麼？

ans 介系詞，用來表達「物體間的空間關係」，例如：椅子、衣櫥等實質的東西；也可以表達抽象的事物。人類透過想像力，將空間的概念比喻到事物上，與抽象的事物（時間）以及情感（好心情）做連結，因此引申出很多意涵。

♠ 以抽象的時間來說：

There is a press conference on Tuesday.

（星期二有一場記者會。）

♠ 以抽象的情緒來說：

When the situation presented itself, I felt the mood of everyone in the room became down.

（當事情浮出檯面，我感覺房內大家的心情都變差了。）

Q₂：介系詞怎麼學？

ans 介系詞很常見，出現時卻又不是你理解的那個意思。你可能會想，介系詞到底有沒有規律可循？介系詞其實難在它的一字多義，而當你先知道基礎的「空間意涵」，再來了解「引申意涵」，接著進而用片語的模式來理解「與介系詞一同出現的搭配詞」，相信你一定會對介系詞有更近一步的了解。

♠ 重點 1：從「語意」來習得

本書將會一一介紹常見、實用的介系詞，並從中……

(1) 了解介系詞的空間意涵（spatial meaning）。

(2) 了解介系詞從空間引申的語意（metaphorical meaning）或其他。

♠ 重點 2：從「介系詞的搭配詞」來記憶與理解

1. 與動詞連用的介系詞：「動詞＋介系詞」

(1) You can count on me.

（你可以依靠我。）

(2) Never lie to yourself.

（絕不要對自己說謊。）

(3) The flight departs from Terminal 1.

（那班飛機從第一航廈起飛。）

2. 與形容詞連用的介系詞：「連綴動詞＋形容詞＋介系詞」

(1) Follow the six steps, and you'll be free from debt.

（照著這六個步驟，你就可以無貸一身輕了。）

(2) She is not satisfied with his answer.

（她對他的答案不滿意。）

(3) He has become dependent on sleeping pills.

（他已經變得依賴安眠藥了。）

3. 與名詞連用的介系詞：「介系詞＋名詞＋介系詞」

(1) The charity collects used books on behalf of the uneducated.

（那間慈善機構以那些沒有接受教育的人們的名義來收集舊書刊。）

(2) In view of the sacrifice his sister made, he bought a car for her.

（考量到他姊姊所做的犧牲，他買了一部車給她。）

(3) For public schools which are in favor of English, their native language courses are removed.

（某些地區的公立中學將母語課程移除，以支持英語的培養。）

4. **複合詞：介系詞與動詞、名詞、形容詞等結合，形成獨立的單字，同時也包含該介系詞原本的空間意涵。**

(1) 有「向上」意涵的 up

upgrade *(v.)* 提升、提高

upcoming *(adj.)* 即將來臨的

upscale *(adj.)* 高端的

(2) 有「在……之上」意涵的 over

overreact *(v.)* 反應過度

overcome *(v.)* 克服、戰勝

overall *(adj./adv.)* 整體來説

(3) 有「在……之下」意涵的 under

underestimate *(v.)* 低估

undergone *(v.)* 經歷

undergraduate *(n.)* 大學生（在大學體系中修讀第一個學位，也就是學士。）

註　上列的 scale、all 單字為名詞。

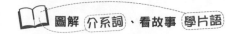

Q3：介系詞在句子中的作用是什麼？

ans 在句子中扮演提供「詳細資訊」的角色，表達句子中「動作者」與「環境」的關係，例如：上下、前後、左右的「方向關係」或是「移動路線」。動作者在本書中又稱作「物體 A」，環境又稱「物體 B」。

♠ 表達物體移動的「軌跡」；表達物體移動時的「終點」。

The flea flew from the woman's clothes into the morning sunlight.

（跳蚤從那女人的衣服上飛到早晨的陽光中。）

♠ 表達物體的「位置」。

The woman is cleaning in the yard.

（那個女人在院子中清掃。）

解析

如果把兩個介系詞片語拿掉，這個句子就顯得資訊很少，並沒有辦法得知跳蚤到哪去了，或是女人在哪裡清掃，但是有了介系詞片語就更能了解動作者與環境的關係，達到清楚溝通的目的。

Q4：既然介系詞表達「物體移動的路徑與方向」，主詞一定都要是會動的生命嗎？

ans 介系詞表達物體的「方向」，不管物體有沒有實際移動，我們的內心都會腦補，給抽象、沒有生命的事物，一個移動的路線。

我們可從介系詞與動詞的搭配中知悉一二，動詞可以簡單分兩種，看完下列例子，你會發現例句 1、2 中的動作者 key、lecture 是沒有生命的、抽象的事物，而例句 3 中的動作者 the cat，才是有生命，可以「自行移動的個體」。

♠ 連綴動詞：is、am、are

(1) Your key is right at the bottom of the jar.

（你的鑰匙就在罐子下面。）

♠ 一般動詞：look、throw、leap、go、get

(2) The lecture was so difficult that it all went over my head.

（那堂課好難，我根本全部都聽不懂。）

(3) The cat leaps at the mouse.

（那隻貓跳向那隻老鼠。）

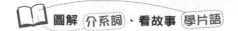
♠ 給沒有生命的事物腦補路線的情況如下：試著想想一個老外跟你說他們國家的國民笑話，你卻一點也聽不懂，這時這則笑話，就像一顆球一樣，從你頭上匆匆飛過不留痕跡。

The joke goes over my head.

（我聽不懂這則笑話。）

 片語補給站

go over one's head 某事因為太過複雜，而讓人無法理解

Q5：介系詞的有幾種？

ans 聽到介系詞，應該會馬上聯想到國高中的課本中所介紹的 in、out、on、at、up、down 等等表達「位置」的介系詞，但這些只是介系詞中一部分而已，從「文法的詞類分類」來學習，介系詞可以分為四種：

♠ 單詞介系詞 (simple prepositions)

「單詞」就是一個字，一個字的介系詞，例如：in、out、on、at、up、upon、down、on、off、with、within、without、by、against、before、after、over、above、behind、below、away、across、around、through、about、form、of、for。

♠ 分詞介系詞 (participial prepositions)

「分詞」即由動詞加字尾 -ed 或是 -ing 而形成的，而「分詞介系詞」，就是由特定的動詞轉換成分詞，擔任介系詞角色的詞類，例如：assuming、concerning、considering、including、, regarding……等。

♠ 片語介系詞 (phrasal prepositions)

「片語」是由字串所組成的，通常由 2 ~ 3 個字所形成，片語中一定含有一個以上的「單詞介系詞」，例如：according to、along with、apart from、because of、except for、next to、owing to、together with、up to、down to。

♠ 介系詞副詞化 (adverbial prepositions)

介系詞作副詞用修飾動詞，即為「副詞化」，而其語意還是引申自原本的的空間關係，例如：You should move on. 你應該往前看（生活還是要過）。

Q6：學語言只要查字典翻譯就可以了嗎？

ans 學習語言不是只查字典就可以了，這要從字典意義與文化上的語意來探討。語意相同卻在不同類型的文體中，有不同的使用狀況，即為「字典意義」與「文化意涵」的差異，你可以想像兩個不同的人，表達相同情緒，卻使用不同用語時的狀況：

表達當某事發生時，覺得好玩又趣的心情，一個身穿蘿莉裝的女孩說：「真有趣！」；另一個理工宅男吃著餅乾打電動時說：「真是太有意思了！」，其中的差別在於：一群相同背景的人，例如蘿莉女孩與其他女孩們，在聊天中因為背景相似，對於一句話所想到的畫面跟情緒連結都會相似，這時蘿莉女孩與理工宅男就分別代表了不同的文化族群。

運用相同的概念，請比較 despite（儘管）與 in spite of（儘管），即使兩者在字典上的意思相同，但有些人認為，in spite of 因為本身字數較多，較冗長（wordy），在強調精簡的正式寫作中比較少用，例如：學術文章，而較常在官僚用語、法律文件、口語時出現。

PART **1**

圖解介系詞篇

♠ 談到空間關係時，to 表達「物體間方向性」，中文意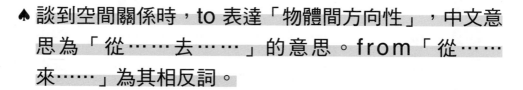思為「從……去……」的意思。from「從……來……」為其相反詞。

關鍵例句

Mary walks to the kitchen and opens the refrigerator.

（瑪莉走到廚房並打開冰箱。）

解析

「動作＋ to ＋ 地點」表示了動作的路徑與終點。

關於 **to** 這個介系詞

♠ 表達「附加……上」的 to

「apply... to（塗抹到……上）」的 to 表達物體 A「接觸」到物體 B。

Apply the lotion to your body.

（將乳液塗抹到身體上。）

♠ 表達「比較」的 to

「A is superior to B（某 A 較某 B 更好）」的 to「比較」物體 A 與物體 B。

Riley's acting talent is far superior to her brother's.

（萊利的演戲天份比她的哥哥還要好。）

♠ 表達「進入下一個事件」的 to

「a way/key to success（成功的關鍵）」的 to 也是表達「進入到下一個狀態」，例如從菜鳥的階段「進入成功的老鳥」階段。

Your brilliant idea is a way to success.

（你的絕佳主意是通往成功之路。）

解析

請想像抵達另一個地方，又是一個故事的開始，to 表達「進入下一個事件」，可以搭配一般動詞或是連綴動詞。

♠ 表達「進入某個人的生命中」的 to

「came to one's aid 幫助某人」的 to 表達「來到我的生活中提供幫助」，例如在路上協助銀髮族過馬路。

My best friend came to my aid.

（我最好的朋友來幫我。）

解析

這時可以想像很多偶像劇常會有的台詞：「謝謝你來到我的生命中」（Thank you for coming into my life.）。這個時候，我們要把每個人的人生之旅想成「一個罐子」，進入了一個人的生命，發展一段關係，如家人、情侶、至交，都不是隨便可以離開的，所以會使用表示「進入一個空間中的 into」。

介系詞的超級比一比

♠ 表達「移動方向的」的 to 與 at

at 強調了某事件發生的「特定的座標位置」，to 則是表達事件／物體「的方向」，但有時候兩者是可以交替使用的，但要留意其語意是有些微的差異的。

The naughty boy threw the ball to his sister.

The naughty boy threw the ball at his sister.

（那個頑皮的男孩，把球丟向她的妹妹。）

解析

throw at 與 throw to 的用法均可表達物體「移動的方向」，但是 throw at 因為表達的位置更為精確，為一個「點」的概念，因此在語意上更有「針對性、攻擊性」。

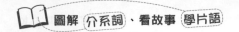
 介系詞 to 小學堂

♠ 練習：請選出適當的片語，分別填入下列空白處。

are married to
trying to
expected to
happened to

❶ Riley and Ben _____ each other.

❷ For Ryan, the best thing that _____ him was that he was paid to hike the Rocky Mountain.

❸ Don't be mad at your father. He is just _____ get to know you more.

❹ She has never _____ be an expert in a few months.

PART 1 圖解介系詞篇

PART 2 看故事學片語篇

解答

❶ are married to 與……結婚。

萊利與班結婚了。

解析：「**be married to somebody** 與……結婚」的 **to** 表達物體 **A** 與物體 **B** 不僅有接觸，並「結為一體」。

❷ happened to 發生在某人身上。

對萊恩來說，有人付他錢去爬洛磯山脈真是有史以來最好的事了。

❸ be trying to 試著要達成某事，**to** 表達「目的」。

別生你爸的氣了，他只是想要試著更了解你而已。

❹ expected to 期待……。

她從來不敢期待可以在幾個月內成為專家。

from

♠ 談到空間關係時，from 表達「物體間方向性」，中文意思為「從……來……」的意思。to「從……去……」為其相反詞。

關鍵例句

The seagull flew from its nest to the beach.

（海鷗從他的巢飛到海灘。）

The heavy mental music came from the water park.

（重金屬音樂是從水上樂園傳出來的。）

關於 **from** 這個介系詞

♠ 表達「源頭」的概念

「A is from B（來自於……）」

My parents are from Oregon.

（我的父母來自奧勒岡州。）

解析

> 由於 from 表達源頭。在 My parents are from Oregon. 或是 Where are you from? 兩個句子中，from 的語意不只有「你從哪裡來」，還包含了「你的家鄉是哪裡？」。

♠ 表達「度量衡的一個區間」概念，例如：時間、溫度、金錢等「range from A to B（介於……區間）」

The climate has changed dramatically year by year. It can be told from the great temperature difference between the day and night time ranging from ten to twenty degrees Celsius.

（氣候變遷逐年越加劇烈。這樣的變化從極大的日夜溫差可看出，日夜溫度相差幅度為攝氏 10 度至 20 度間。）

♠ 表達「來源」，例如：字體的來源、消息的來源、材料的來源等「derive from（源自於……）」

"Blogs" are also known as weblogs, deriving from two words: web and log.

（部落格（blogs）又稱作網誌（weblogs），其說法是來自於英文 web（網頁）和 blog（日誌）這兩個字。）

♠ 「benefit from（從……中獲得好處）」

The teachers have seen that some students benefit from thoughtful planning of teaching, such as setting up learning targets and giving career directions.

（教師們看著學生們從縝密的教學規劃中獲得好處，例如設定學習目標以及生涯規劃。）

介系詞的超級比一比

♠ 比較：out of「從……出來」、from「從……來」

The woman and her daughters are from Pakistan.

（那個女人跟她的女兒們來自巴基斯坦。）

解析

例句中的 from Pakistan 可以有兩個意思，一為家鄉為巴基斯坦，二為上一個停留之地是巴基斯坦，端看說話者或前後文的文意來推斷。

The woman and her daughters are out of Pakistan.

（那個女人跟她的女兒們終於離開巴基斯坦了。）

解析

out of 強調「離開某一個邊界」，邊界可以是一個國家、一個難纏的事件等，例句中使用 out of 可能隱含母女好不容易離開這個可能會造成生命危險的國家。

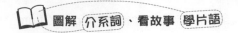

 介系詞 from 小學堂

♠ 練習：請選出適當的片語，分別填入下列空白處

learned from
a few miles from
heard from
suffered from

❶ What I _____ those entrepreneurs is their attitude toward life. They work hard and dream big.

❷ Mom complained that she had not _____ Jeffrey in years. She has no idea where he'd gone.

❸ Her house is only _____ your place.

❹ The man who _____ cancer feels hopeless towards life.

解答

① learned from 從……中學到。

我在那些企業家身上所學到的是他們的人生態度，他們努力工作勇敢作夢。

② heard from 有……人的消息。

母親抱怨她已經好幾年沒有聽到傑佛瑞的消息了，她完全不知道他去了哪裡。

解析：「hear from＋人」表達聽到某人的消息。

③ a few miles from... 距離某處幾英里。

她家離你家不過幾英里而已。

解析：「距離 ＋ from ＋ 地方」表達距離某處多遠。

④ suffered from 受……之苦。

那位飽受癌症之苦的男人覺得人生沒有希望了。

♠ 談到 in 所表達的空間關係時，in 為「在……之內」
的意思，表達「物體」被限制在「特定空間」中，一
個 3D 的立體空間。

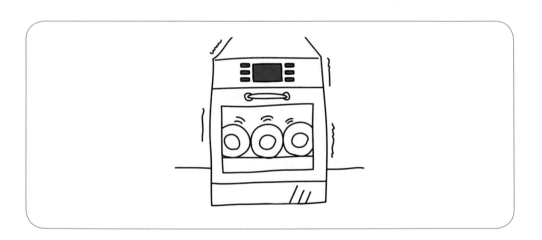

關鍵例句

The plates are in a dish washing machine.

（盤子在洗碗機中。）

解析

想像「東西」在「容器」裡，是一種東西被「侷限在特定空間
中」的概念，有時候表達不能輕易可以離開的概念，也就是英文
containment（控制）是意思。

動詞和介系詞 in 來配對

♠ 「in prison（坐牢）」，in＋事物、地方，表達思緒、情感、行為被侷限了

The serial killer is in prison.

（連環殺手進監獄了。）

解析

> 監獄代表一個「特定空間」，而處在其中的「連環殺手」因為犯了罪，而必須待在「監獄裡」，並不能想離開就離開，行為被「限制」了。

♠ 「in＋language（透過某種語言溝通）」，in 表達透過某物完成某事

She speaks in English.

（她用英文來溝通。）

解析

> 她用說話來達成溝通的目的，而溝通的達成，需要靠英文這個語言來執行，此溝通工具，已「限定為英文」。

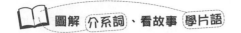
♠「be in love（戀愛了）」表達「思想上、情感上陷入其中」的概念

William is in love.

（威廉戀愛了。）

解析

戀愛中的人，會將愛情寄託在另一個人身上，這種感情不是能輕易抽離的，因此使用表達「限定在某空間中」的介系詞 in。

♠「participate in（參與）」

After the workshop, many of my colleagues are eager to participate in the similar activities in the future.

（工作坊結束後，很多我同事熱切期待未來參與類似的活動。）

♠「be born in（出生於）」後面可接某個時代或是地點

If you were born in the 19th century, you could expect to receive handwritten letters.

（如果你在 19 世紀出生，你可以期待收到手寫的信。）

介系詞的超級比一比

♠ 比較「在哪裡」的 in 與 on

in 所表達之空間是有限制性的，物體較難輕易移動，而 on 所表達的空間是一個具有支撐性的，不具限制性，物體可以輕易移動的。

The candy is in the jar.

（糖果在罐子中。（瓶口小，狹窄難拿的。））

The candy is on the table.

（糖果在桌面上。（2D 的開放空間，可以輕易拿取。））

♠ 比較：表達「在……中」的 in 以及表達「在……之下」的 under

❶ Jamie is in the pool.

（潔咪在游泳池中。）

解析

in 表達身體的某個部份泡在水中，潔咪可能只有泡腳，或是站在游泳池中頭頂露出。

❷ Ariel is under the sea.

（艾莉兒在水裡。）

解析

under 表示身體的每個部分都在水裡，包括頭、手、腳等，是「完全在……之中」，英文意思為 completely in。

45

練習：請選出適當的片語，分別填入下列空白處。

> in August
> has... in sights
> in this book
> in sickness
> in... outfit

❶ When the hunter _____ a rabbit _____, he fires.

❷ Mary opens a love letter from Peter, the line says, "I will stand by you _____ or in health, in poverty, or in wealth."

❸ The lady _____ Gucci _____ looks fabulous.

❹ Peter and Mary are getting married _____.

❺ Every information I learned about camping is written _____.

解答

❶ has... in sights 瞄準某物。

當獵人鎖定兔子時，他就開槍。

解析：in sights 跟 keep in touch（保持聯絡）的 in 均表達感
　　　官的可及性，也就是視野所及之意。

❷ in sickness 生病了。

瑪麗打開彼得給她的情書，裡面這樣寫著：「不論生病或健康、
富裕或貧窮，我都會在你的身邊。」

❸ in... outfit 著某種服裝。

那個身穿古馳服裝的女人容光煥發。

❹ in August 在八月。

彼得與瑪麗八月就要結婚了。

解析：in 在此為表達時間的介系詞，「in＋month 在某個月
　　　份」。

❺ in this book 在這本書裡面。

我所學任何關於露營的資訊都寫在本書中。

解析：介系詞 in 在這邊的概念是，你的思想被這本書限制
　　　（containment）著，因為你正在閱讀他、消化其中的意
　　　思。

on

♠ 談到 on 所表達的空間關係時，on 為「在……之上」的意思，表達「物體」在一個平面的 2D 空間上，強調物體間的接觸。其相反詞為 off，表達「離開……」的意思。

關鍵例句

You can mount your camera on the wall.

（你可以將攝影機安裝在牆壁上。）

You can also install your camera on the ceiling with optional supporting rack.

（你也可以選購支架將攝影機安裝在天花板上。）

解析

on 表達「物體」與「支撐該物體的空間」之關係，是一個「面」的概念，也就是 2D 空間。請想像攝影機安裝在天花板上、牆上，機器與牆壁是「有接觸的」，而牆壁扮演了「支撐機器」的一個「面」。

動詞和介系詞 on 來配對

♠ 「based on（根據）」根據一個資料來源，再加以延伸其概念。可以想像你是一位作家，想要將你的人生經歷寫成一本小說，這時候你會在紙上開始描繪一些人生經歷，整理成一份大綱。這樣就跟前面所提到的「2D 的平面」不謀而合了。

The story is based on the author's experiences in childhood.

（這個故事是改編自作者的童年。）

♠ 「come on（過來、來吧！）」可以表達實際上的「朝某方向移動」，或是用「移動吧！過來吧！」這類祈使句，來「鼓勵別人採取行動」。

Come on; be brave.

（就放手去做，勇敢點！）

Come on, doggie.

（小狗狗過來。）

♠ 「focus on（重點放在……）」在一個平面上聚焦，讓重點凸顯。

In our last discussion, we focused on the following salient features.

在我們上次的討論中，我們專注在下列的顯著特徵。

♠ 「be on the pill 避孕」

She is on the pill.

（她有在避孕。）

解析

❶ 避孕這件事情是當事人的選擇，當其決定不避孕時，隨時可以停藥，因此介系詞使用表達「平面、開放空間的 on」而非「在限定的空間中的 in」。

❷ 在美式英文中，on the pill 其實就是 on the birth control pill 的意思，因為這種比較隱私的事情一般不會在對話中明說，因此用 on the pill 表示。

介系詞的超級比一比

♠ 比較表達「在⋯⋯之上」的 on 與 onto

on 表達「接觸」，onto 則是「力的接觸」，例如：
作用力，或是抽象的努力。

The dog accidentally crashed onto our roof.

（那隻小狗意外地跌倒在我們家的屋頂。）

I don't see how John can hang onto his job.

（我不知道強尼要怎麼繼續他的工作。）

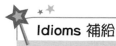

Idioms 補給

hang onto / hang on to 堅持某事、持續做某事

 介系詞 **on** 小學堂

♠ 練習：請選出適當的片語，分別填入下列空白處。

on my way
rely on
on purpose
on the go
work on

❶ Dad! You did it _____.

❷ Home sweet home. I am _____ home.

❸ The more you _____ it, the more confidence you get as you do it.

❹ He has been _____ it all day long.

❺ Qualcomm and Broadcom are competitors, and at the same time they _____ each other's techniques to develop new products.

解答

❶ on purpose 故意的。

爸！你是故意這麼做的。

解析：**on** 這邊隱含著基礎（basis）的意涵，也就是題目中老爸做某件事是基於另一件事情。

❷ on my way 在去某地的路上。

家，可愛的家，我已經在回家的路上了。

❸ work on... 從事於 ……。

你越去做那件事，你就會越來越有自信。

❹ on the go 非常忙碌。

他已經忙碌一整天了。

❺ rely on 依賴。

高通與博通為彼此競爭的公司，同時他們也仰賴彼此的技術開發新產品。

（側邊標籤）

PART 1 圖解介系詞篇

PART 2 看故事學片語篇

♠ at 表達「物體在某個地點」，當物體在行進中時，停下來的那個「地點」就是使用 at 的時機，是一種座標的概念，用來表達物體位於「某個點上」。

關鍵例句

Miley went on a road trip and stopped at New Jersey.

（麥莉開始公路旅行，並且在紐澤西駐足。）

Mitch is at the pharmacy.

（米契在藥局。）

解析

使用 at 強調人在那個地方，是一種座標的概念，也因此 at the pharmacy 並沒有指明是在藥局裡，還是藥局門口。但如果我們說 Mitch is in the pharmacy，這時很明顯他的人是在藥局裡面。

關於 at 這個介系詞

♠ 表達動作者位於哪裡時，at 與 in 的使用差別在於：

➤「at＋店名（專有名詞）」

Mitch is at the Ambassador.

（米契在國賓影城。）

♠「in＋某種建築物名稱」，因為建築物有四面牆，有密閉空間，因此使用 in。

Mitch is in the theater.

（米契在電影院裡。）

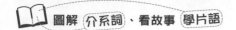

 ## 動詞和介系詞 at 來配對

♠ 「aim at（目標是達成……）」，表達動作者心之所嚮，也就是目的。

This is a basic course aiming at improving student's understanding for more advanced subjects later.

（這是一門基礎課程，目的是要改善學生的理解力，以利未來的進階課程。）

♠ 「be good at guessing（擅長猜測……）」，使用「be bad at / be good at＋動詞」表達專精／不擅長做某事。

If no one can figure out the answer, ask Anna. She is good at guessing.

（如果沒有人知道答案是什麼，問安娜就對了。她很會猜。）

♠ 「laugh at（嘲笑某人）」，表達引起某種情緒的原因。

No offense. But you've got to be able to laugh at yourself.

（沒有針對你，但是你必須要能夠笑看自己的所作所為。）

♠ 「be at work（在工作）」，表達動作者目前的狀態。

The boy hesitates when knocking his father's door because his father is at work.

（男孩在敲父親的房門時猶豫了一下，因為他的父親正在工作。）

♠ 「at one's convenience（在某人方便的時候）」，表達動作者目前的狀態。

When can you come by? I would like to have you to taste some homemade food at your convenience.

（你何時可以過來我家？你方便的時候，我希望你可以來嚐嚐一些自製的食物。）

介系詞 **at** 小學堂

♠ 練習：請選出適當的片語，分別填入下列空白處。

at your service
glanced at
at rest
arrived at
is bad at

❶ We are sorry for your lost. Princess Mia is now lying _____ in her family's vault.

❷ Kate _____ saying no which gets herself in trouble a lot.

❸ I'll be _____, my lord.

❹ The daughter _____ her mother swiftly and saw the concern on her face.

❺ James _____ the hospital the earliest.

解答

❶ at rest 安息、死亡。

請節哀，蜜雅公主現在安息在她們家族的墓室中。

解析：at 表達動作者目前的狀態，當人永遠休息時就是死亡，當
不想說出「死亡」的字眼時，可以用 at rest 來做替換。

❷ is bad at 不擅長於……。

凱特很不會拒絕別人，常常為自己惹上麻煩。

❸ at your service 為您效勞。

我的主人，我願為您效勞。

❹ glanced at 匆匆瞥一眼。

女兒往媽媽的臉上匆匆瞥一眼，就看到她臉上的擔心。

❺ arrived at 抵達某地。

詹姆士最早抵達醫院。

out

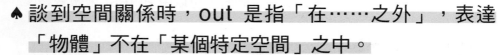

♠ 談到空間關係時，out 是指「在……之外」，表達「物體」不在「某個特定空間」之中。

關鍵例句

He takes a pen out of his pencil box.

（他把筆從鉛筆盒中拿出來。）

解析

將「筆」從「鉛筆盒中」拿出來，即表達出這隻筆的「可取得性」，也就是英文中 accessibility 這個字；筆可以隨意取用，而不是被限制著，即為 non-containment 的概念，恰好與 in 表達出相反的空間概念。

They will eat out last night.

（他們明晚會出去吃。）

解析

　　out 表達「某物」不在其「預設存在的位置」，在家裡吃飯是較為稀鬆平常的事情，可解釋為預設之行為；而出去吃，則可能是因為某人生日才特地安排的行為，為「非預設之意」。

 動詞和介系詞 out 來配對

♠「out of something（某物用光了）」，表達「完畢了」，可以指東西用完了，或是事情完成了。

We are out of milk. Get some at the grocery store.

（我們沒有牛奶了。到雜貨店買一些吧。）

The poor girl is out of luck.

（那可憐的女孩運氣很差。）

♠ 「dry out（吹乾、弄乾）」指將水分子移除到某物體之外的這個動作完成了。

You need to dry out your hair before you go to bed.

（你一定要在睡前把頭髮吹乾。）

解析

頭髮中的「水分」離開「頭髮」，也就是「某物」不在「某個空間中」的意義延伸。

♠ 「figure out（想出辦法）」out 表達事情的解決方法已經顯露出來了，也就解決了一個難題。

We figured out the problem.

（我們解決了這個問題。）

 介系詞 **out** 其它應用

♠ 表達「由中心點四散開來」的 out

➤ 「spread out 平均塗抹」

He spreads out the jelly on the toast.

（他把果醬塗抹到吐司上。）

➤ 「hand something out... 將……拿出來分配」

The teacher handed the test papers out.

（老師將考試卷發下去。）

♠ 表達「不在某處」的 out

➤ 「keep out 遠離」，表達「排除在……之外」。

Keep out of the restricted area.

（遠離限制的區域。）

➤ 「out of sight（不在身邊）」，表達人與人之間的情感，若不在身邊（在視線之外）自然就不在心上了。

Out of sight, out of mind.

（眼不見，心不想。）

介系詞 out 小學堂

♠ 練習：請選出適當的片語，分別填入下列空白處。

sort things out
turn out
go out
bursts out crying
stretch out

❶ Katie is grounded. She can't _____ clubbing with you girls.

❷ The butterfly pose can _____ the inner thighs.

❸ The coffee shop is where I can think, focus, and _____ .

❹ Whenever Emma faces difficulty, she _____ .

❺ Emily is so naive that she believes everything will _____well.

解答

❶ go out 出去玩（離開家去外面走走）。

凱蒂被禁足了，她不能跟你們女孩去夜店玩了。

❷ stretch out 伸展。

蝴蝶式可以伸展大腿內側。

❸ sort things out 解決問題、整理思緒。

咖啡店是一個我可以思考、專注、解決問題的空間。

❹ bursts out crying 放聲大哭。

每當艾瑪遇到困難，她就放聲大哭。

❺ turn out 結果是。

艾蜜莉太天真了，她相信每件事情都會圓滿收場。

off

♠ 談到 off 所表達的的空間關係時，off 為「不在……某平面上」的意思，強調物體間的分離（separation）。其相反詞為強調接觸（contact）的 on「在……之上」。

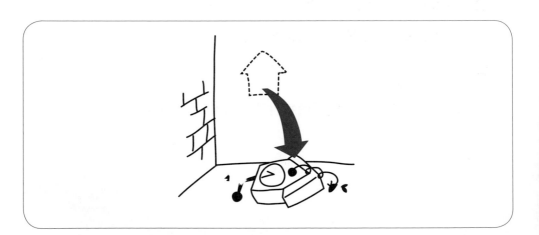

關鍵例句

The antique clock fell off the wall when the earthquake hits Taiwan.

（當地震襲來臺灣時古老的鐘從牆上掉下來。）

Keep off the wet paint.

（油漆未乾、勿碰。）

關於 **off** 這個介系詞

♠ 表達「離開某物的表面」的 off

➢ 「take off something / take something off 脫掉」

Annie: We are looking for a boarder.

Rob: Hopefully a female. Girls keep their room tidy.

Annie: A male is also fine. But he had better take off his shoes when he comes inside.

安妮：我們在找一位寄宿生。

羅伯：希望是女生，女孩們會保持整潔。

安妮：男生也可以啦，只是他最好要在進門前脫鞋子。

♠ 表達「讓人討厭地倒彈」的 off，既然討厭了自然不會想接近、只想保持距離。

➢ 「piss somebody off 讓某人……討厭」

The lady who cut in line pissed others in line off.

（那位插隊的女子讓排隊的其他人覺得生氣。）

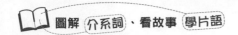

♠ 表達「停止運作」的 off，強調東西不能使用、無法取得服務（inaccessibility）：

➤ 「turn off something / turn something off 將電器的電源關閉」

Annie: Do you know where Mike is?

Rob: I don't know. He has turned his cell phone off. I've left a dozen messages.

安妮：你知道麥可在哪嗎？

羅伯：我不知道，他把他的手機關機了。我已經留了好多通留言。

➤ 「off duty 下班／休假」

The police officer was officially off duty for the rest of the weekend.

（那位警察接下來這週都不用執勤。）

介系詞的超級比一比

♠ **比較：on 表達「可以取得的」、off 表達「無法取得的」**

在餐廳中，某道甜點、菜餚的上架與下架可以這麼說：

Be off the menu 某道菜有供應

Be on the menu 某道菜沒有供應

The mango pudding is off now because it is out of the season during the winter, but our strawberry pie is available now.

（因為冬天不是芒果的產季，芒果布丁已經不供應了，但是我們目前有草莓派。）

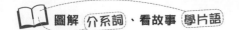

介系詞 **off** 小學堂

♠ 練習：請選出適當的片語，分別填入下列空白處。

better off
pays off
off topic
switches off
sold off

❶ The man creates a strategic spending plan and soon he _____ his debt.

❷ The woman always _____ the light before she leaves the room.

❸ The comment Paul made was completely _____.

❹ Her ex-husband is a fool. She is _____ without him.

❺ After the divorce, she _____ the furniture and gave away half her jewelry.

解答

❶ pays off 償還……。

那個男人自創了一套花費戰略後，很快地他就還完他的貸款了。

❷ switches off 將裝置關掉。

那個女人總是會在離開房間前將燈關掉。

❸ off topic 不恰當、不相關。

保羅的評論實在離題了。

❹ better off 較佳的、較明智的。

她的前夫是傻子，她沒有他過得更好。

❺ sold off 賣光。

離婚過後，她賣掉她所有的傢俱，並把她一半的珠寶贈送出去。

up、down

♠ up 表達「方向往上」，up 在物理上表達上升之意，如電梯往上。down 表達「方向向下」，down 在物理上表達下降之意。

圖 1　up	圖 2　down

關鍵例句

Jessie climbed up the hill.

（潔西爬上山丘。）

Winter is coming. All the leaves are falling down.

（冬天來了，所有葉子都掉下來了。）

關於 **up** 和 **down** 這兩個介系詞

♠ **up** 用來表達「物體 A 靠近物體 B」的一個移動路徑，是英文中的 approach 之意。**down** 則為「由 A 處往 B 處」的移動，移動不一定看得到，視線的移動就是一種。A 在這裡的地理、社會的位置較高。

A good-looking stranger comes up to me and asks me out.

（一位帥氣的陌生人向我走來，還約我出去。）

This is a perfect place to look down upon the whole town.

（這裡是能俯瞰整座城鎮好地方。）

介系詞 **up** 和 **down** 其它應用

♠ **up** 生活應用之表達「更多、更好」、**down** 則表達「更少、更差」：

➤ 「turn up the heat 打開暖爐」，turn up 為打開裝置之意，up 表達在數量或質量上「更多」之意，在這裡表達溫度的升高。

Anna: It's cold outside but warm inside.

Tyler: The heat was turned up a while ago.

安娜：外面好冷，裡面好溫暖。

泰勒：暖爐稍早就打開了。

➤ 「dress up 盛裝打扮」，up 與動詞連用，表達「改善」之意。

Mom: My birthday girl, you have to dress up.

Daughter: I don't think so.

媽媽：妳今天生日，要打扮一下。

女兒：不用啦。

➤ 「slim down 變瘦了」，down 表達在數量或質量上「更少」之意。

After going on a diet for months, Luke has slimmed down.

（經過幾個月的節食，路克變瘦了。）

➤ 「be down 情況變差」，例如經濟狀況變差、體力變差。

The Brown family is down on luck. They are now homeless.

（伯朗一家很不幸，他們現在無家可歸。）

Dad is down with the flu.

（父親得了流感病倒了。）

♠ up 和 down 生活應用之表達「完成了、用完了」：

➤ 「fill up 裝滿」，up 與動詞連用，水壺裝滿了，也代表該動作之完成。

The waitress fills up the pitcher with water.

（服務員將水壺裝滿水。）

➤ 「finish up 完成某事、對某事做最後努力」

Let's finish up this work and go home.

（我們來完成今天的工作然後回家吧。）

➤ 「drink up 喝光光」，up 與動詞連用，表達「消耗完畢」之意。

We drank up all the wine from the cellar.

（我們喝完了所有酒窖中的葡萄酒。）

➤ 「down to wire 時間剩下最後一刻」，down 隱含「資源消耗完了」之意，這邊解釋為時間所剩不多。

Our team is down to wire with the project.

（能完成這個案子的時間不多了。）

 介系詞 **up** 和 **down** 小學堂

♠ 練習：請選出適當的片語，分別填入下列空白處。

keep up	slow down
is up	calm down
picked up	has gone down
showing up	shut down
is still up	go down

❶ The project can't be closed now because everything _____ in the air.

❷ Time _____. No more talking, please.

❸ A strong wind flew through, _____ the fallen leaves, and swirled them around.

❹ The parents are frightened when they see their kids _____ with a gun in the house.

❺ I hate to hear my boss saying: " _____ the great work, Tony!"

❻ The tourists watched the sun _____ at Pier 39.

❼ You are getting too excited. Try to _____.

❽ The gas price _____ recently. It's the best timing to buy flight tickets.

❾ People wondered who _____ the company?

❿ Don't ask me to hurry up. If you do so, I would just _____.

解答

❶ is still up 事情還在進行。

這個案子尚未結束,因為都還在進行著。

解析:**something is up** 與 **what's up** 的 up 均表達「事件的出現或是進行」,隱含著「尚未安定」的意思,英文為 **unsettledness**。

❷ is up 結束。

時間到了，請不要再説話了。

❸ picked up 撿起（往上帶起之意）。

一陣強風吹過，將落葉從地上捲起。

❹ showing up 出現。

當父母看到他們的孩子帶著一把槍出現在家裡時，他們嚇壞了。
解析：**up** 表達靠近、接近，因為接近了，所以進入了視線之內。

❺ keep up 維持、保持。

我討厭聽到老闆跟我説：「繼續維持這麼棒的工作，東尼！」

❻ go down 落下。

遊客在 39 號碼頭看夕陽。

❼ calm down 冷靜。

你太激動了，試著冷靜一下。

❽ has gone down 價格下跌。

油價最近下跌了，現在是最好買機票的時機。

❾ shut down 關閉。

人們好奇是誰關閉了那間公司？

❿ slow down 放慢腳步。

不要叫我快一點，如果你這麼做，我只會放慢步調而已。

over、under

♠ 談到「物體的移動路徑時」，over 表達穿越其上、
under 表達穿越其下

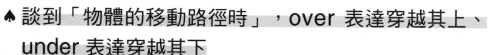
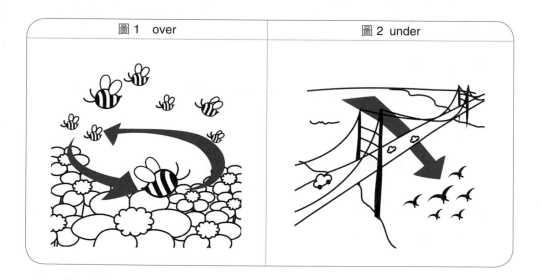

| 圖 1　over | 圖 2　under |

關鍵例句

Hundreds of bees are hovering over the blooming flowers.

（一大群蜜蜂在盛開的花朵上盤旋。）

A flock of birds flew under the Golden Gate Bridge.

（一群鳥兒飛過金門大橋。）

關於 **over** 和 **under** 這兩個介系詞

♠ 談到「物體的空間關係時」，over 表達在其上、under 表達在其下：over 表達「物體 A 在物體 B 之上」的空間關係，under 則表達「物體 A 在物體 B 之下」的空間關係，並隱含物體間兩個「可能會或一定會接觸」，也就是英文中 contact 的意思。

Van Gogh's Starry Night is hung over the mantelpiece.

（梵谷的畫作星空在壁爐台上。）

Your key is right under my chemistry book.

（你的鑰匙就在我的化學課本下面。）

解析

畫作與壁爐兩者的組合影響了房間的外觀，兩者物體間是有「互相影響」之關係在，而非不相干的個體。

介系詞 under 應用

♠ 表達「被罩住」的 under，表示完全在某物之下，那「某物」就引申成保護罩的概念，可以指正面或是負面的事件。

➤ 「Under... circumstance 在某某情況下」

Boss: Under what circumstance would you continue to work for us?

Employee: If I have a raise and get promoted.

老闆：在什麼情況下你願意繼續為我們工作？

員工：加薪與升職。

➤ 「work under pressure 在壓力下工作」

Successful people know how to work under pressure.

（成功的人知道如何在壓力下工作。）

動詞和介系詞 over 來配對

♠ over 表達權力的取回，「某 A」對「某 B」的影響力，有一種「控制」的意涵存在。

➤ take over 接管：權力從 A 處移轉到 B 處的意思。

The king hopes to take over the country without killing

anyone.

（國王希望可以在不殺任何人的情況下接管那個國家。）

➤ get over 克服：以回到原來的狀態、拿回對某事的主導權。

You have to get over your anxiety to speak in English.

（你必須克服你開口說英語的障礙。）

♠ 從 A 地移到 B 地的路徑

➤ come over 過來這：「動作者」從某地過來說話者這邊。

Would you come over to my place and hang out?

（你要過來我家坐坐嗎？）

➤ go over 仔細檢視：「動作者的眼睛」從開始看到結尾，仔細地查看、確認。

Go over your work before you submit it to your boss.

（在繳交你的工作之前，要仔細地確認。）

➤ turn over 翻面：將「目標物」從一邊帶到另一邊，翻面之意。

Turn the fish over and cook the other side.

（把魚翻面，再煮另一邊。）

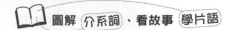
 ## 介系詞 **over** 和 **under**

♠ 練習：請選出適當的片語，分別填入下列空白處。

---

pour... over

win over

under the cover of

hand over

bend over backwards

---

❶ _____ the gravy _____ the mashed potatoes and vegetables.

❷ He _____ the key _____ anyway.

❸ No matter what happens, he is the one who will _____ to help you.

❹ The enemy attacks us _____ a dark night.

❺ With the charm and a glamorous smile, that candidate can _____ working-class voters.

解答

❶ pour something over 將……倒在某物之上。

將肉汁倒在馬鈴薯泥與蔬菜之上。

解析：這句話中你可以想像醬汁從瓶子移動到盤子上的「路徑」，並「覆蓋」在「食物之上」。

❷ hand over 交出。

他還是將鑰匙交出來了。

解析：交出鑰匙同樣有鑰匙從某 A 移到某 B 的路徑，另又涵蓋了「權力移轉」的意思。

❸ bend over backwards 盡全力幫助。

不管發生什麼事情，他一定會盡全力幫助你。

解析：身體直直的往後傾斜，是個辛苦的動作，引申為盡全力幫助別人。

❹ under the cover of... 在……的掩護下。

敵軍在夜色的掩護下攻擊我們。

❺ win over 贏得。

那位候選人有魅力和迷人的微笑，可以贏得勞工階級的選票。

解析：贏得選民的心，是一種「控制」的象徵。

above、below

♠ 談到空間關係時 above 表示「在其上」，below
「在其下」

圖 1　over	圖 2　under
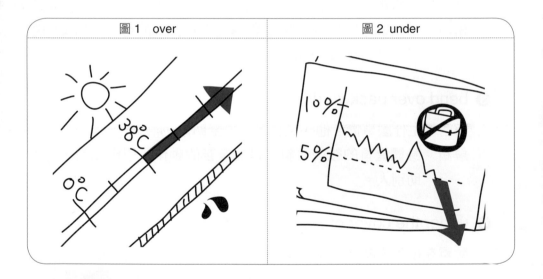	

關鍵例句

The temperature of summer here can rise to above 38°C

（這裡的夏天氣溫可以高到 38 度 C。）

The country' unemployment rate is below 5%.

（這個國家的失業率低於百分之五。）

關於 **above** 和 **below** 這兩個介系詞

♠ above 表達各種事物的「度量衡」較高、較多等；below 則相反。

➤ 表達「物體 A」位於比「物體 B」更高的位置

The building is about 800 meters above the ground.

（這棟建築物距離地面大約 800 尺。）

➤ 表達「物體 A」位於比「物體 B」較低的位置

The whole country is below sea level.

（這整個國家都在海平面之下。）

動詞和介系詞 **above**、**below** 來配對

♠ 「As mentioned above 如上文所述」as mentioned above、as shown above、as listed above、as described above、as stated above 均可以用來表示前面或是上文所提過的事物，這邊的 above、below 用來作副詞用。

This is indeed one of the reasons, as mentioned above so we should take it seriously.

（這的確是其中一個原因，如同前面所述，我們應該要嚴肅對待。）

As described below, teachers may show concern to students'

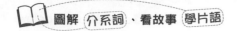

emotional health.

（如同下文所描述的，老師們關注學生的心理健康。）

♠「rank above 排名位於……之前」

In terms of alcohol consumption, Thailand ranked above Taiwan.

（說到酒類的消耗量，泰國較台灣來得高。）

♠「go below 移動至……之下」

The ship is attacked. The captain is going the deck below to check the damage.

（船被魚雷射中了。船長正在走去往下方的甲板，以確認損傷。）

♠「trade below 以低於……的價格交易」

The company's stock has been traded below $12 recently.

（這間公司的股價近期以低於 12 的價錢賣出。）

 介系詞的超級比一比

♠ 本單元的主角 over 與 above 都表達「位置向上」的意思，但兩者有些微的差異：

➤ above 表達「物體 A」在「物體 B」之上，物體是「靜止的」。而說話者也認為兩者「不會有機會接觸」、「也不會互相影響」。

➢ over 表達物體移動之路徑，說話者也認為「物體 A」與「物體 B」是「有接觸」或是「未來有機會接觸」，以及「覆蓋在上」的關係。

♠ 談到物體的「移動路徑」時：

當你要表達鳥兒掠過湖面時，你會搭配介系詞 over：

The bird skims over the lake. (O)

而不會搭配介系詞 above，因為而 skim 這個單字為「掠過」之意，表達「快速的經過表面，有時會接觸到」，自然不會搭配「表達沒有機會接觸的狀況」的介系詞 above:

The bird skims above the lake. (X)

♠ 談到權利時，above 與 over 都可以使用，但其差別在於：

➢ above 表達在「物體 A」沒有直接控制「物體 B」的狀況下，物體 A 較物體 B 優越、具有優先權、或是地位高尚。

In a place where the caste system prevails, the Brahmin believes that their social rank is far above the others.

（在實施種姓制度的地方，婆羅門相信他們比其他人都來得崇高。）

> 註 印度的種姓制度（caste system）是一種社會分級制度（social stratification），將人分成四個等級，從最高到最低的位階分別為：婆羅門、剎帝利、吠舍、首陀羅。

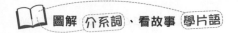

➤ over 表達「物體 A」的權利對於「物體 B」是有潛在的或是直接的影響力。

James is overseeing the new project.

（詹姆士是監督新案子的人。）

 ## 介系詞 **above**、**below** 小學堂

♠ 練習：請選出適當的片語，分別填入下列空白處。

> below the radar
>
> rise above
>
> see above
>
> below the belt

❶ When life is full of craps, _____ craps and speed away.

❷ Behave yourself. That was a little _____ .

❸ The couple are keeping their relationship _____ .

❹ Please _____ for suggestions.

解答

❶ rise above 不受……影響。

當你的人生只剩垃圾時，你必須出淤泥而不染繼續找尋新的人生。

解析：rise above 的用法，呼應了 above 隱含「沒有接觸」的空間關係。

❷ below the belt 言論過於刻薄，羞辱並且不公平的。

請注意你的言行，剛剛那樣太過冒犯了。

❸ stay below the radar 低調進行某事不讓人注意。。

這對情侶不想讓人知道他們正在交往。

❹ see above 見上文（用於書刊、文章中）。

建議的部分請見上文。

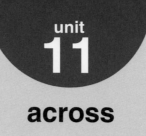

across

♠ across（橫越），與 cross（交叉）屬於同源字，因此也互享了語意，因此 across 的空間關係，也就是一個交叉、十字的形狀。

關鍵例句

The theater is across from the restaurant.

（戲院就在餐廳的對面。）

解析

❶ 當 across 表達空間的位置時，需由「物體 A」與「物體 B」比較才得以表達「在……對面」的意思，視覺上來看就是一個「交叉」。

❷ 英文的表達，還必須加上表達「位置源頭的介系詞 from」，交代是在哪個建築物的對面，形成片語「A is across from B（物體 A 在物體 B 的對面）」。

關於 **across** 這個介系詞

♠ 談到路徑時，across 表達動作者從一邊移動到另一邊（from one side to the other side），以環境來說，動作者「橫越」一片較為「平面的區域」，是 2D 的概念。

關鍵例句

The boy walks across the desert.

（男孩橫越沙漠。）

解析

沙漠是個平面、空曠的區域。

Did you see what just happened? A mouse ran across the kitchen.

（你有看到發生什麼事情嗎？一隻老鼠跑過廚房了。）

解析

對老鼠來說，廚房地板是一個牠可以隨意橫越的平面空間。

 ## 動詞和介系詞 **across** 來配對

♠ across 表達物體穿越的路徑

➤ 「walk / run across＋地方」，指「走」或「跑」的方式「穿越某個平面區域」。

The boy walked across the campus to see the stray dog.

（男孩穿越了整個校園要去看流浪狗。）

 其中的地點也可以替換成：street（街道）、bridge（橋樑）或 playground（遊樂場）。

➤ 「look across＋物體」表達往某物的對面方向

Joy looked across the counter at the man, and she recognized him! He is her lost brother!

（喬伊看著櫃檯對面的男人，她認得他！他就是她走失的弟弟！）

➤ 「a shot across the bows 警告」。在海軍的傳統中，為了警告，會把砲彈射到對方的船頭（bows），後來此一行為比喻「某人做某事以示警告之意」。

The woman's rebellion against social convention is a shot across the bows.

（那個女人對於社會的既有習俗之反叛是她發出的警告。）

♠ across 表達思維在人與人間傳遞的路徑

➤ 「get something across 溝通」：將想法傳遞出去，並且被理解。

The teacher tries to get his points across.

（那位老師試著讓學生理解他的觀點。）

➤ 「splash something across 將……放在引人注目的地方」

The movie reviews were splashed across the front pages of Entertainment Weekly.

（那篇電影回顧被放在娛樂週刊的頭版上。）

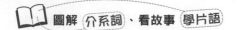

 ## 介系詞 **across** 小學堂

♠ 練習:請選出適當的片語,分別填入下列空白處。

> getting his ideas across
> cut across
> walked across
> driving across
> came across

❶ The man _____ the courtyard.

❷ During a train ride, I _____ a very caring foreigner.

❸ David had a hard time _____ when he was in Mexico.

❹ Don't worry about Lily. She doesn't mind _____ the country by herself.

❺ The boy _____ the Central Park on his way to school.

1
PART

圖解介系詞篇

2
PART

看故事學片語篇

解答

❶ walked across 走過某地。

男人走過庭院。

❷ came across 偶然碰見，在不經意的時候遇到某人、或某事。

坐火車的時候，我遇見一位有愛心的外國人。

❸ getting his ideas across 溝通、將想法傳遞出去。

當大衛在墨西哥的時候，他説的話幾乎無法被理解。

❹ driving across 開車穿越某處。

不用擔心麗麗，她不介意自己開車穿越鄉間。

❺ cut across 走近路。

在去上學的路上，那個男孩穿越中央公園走捷徑。

through

♠ through 穿越。動作者從一個區域中移動到另一個，以環境來說，動作者「穿越立體的空間」，是 3D 的概念。

關鍵例句

The boy walks through an abandoned baseball field.

（男孩穿越一座廢棄的棒球場。）

解析

想像廢棄的棒球場雜草叢生為一個立體的空間，動作者經過此一立體空間時，是被包覆在其中的。

關於 through 這個介系詞

♠ **through** 後面通常會接「表達立體空間的名詞」，例如道路、隧道這種「物體可以通過的特定空間」。

The tunnel through Snow Mountain was finished in 2006.

（雪山隧道在 2006 年時完工。）

I heard that people will easily get lost in the woods unless they find the only one path through.

（我聽説人們會在這片森林迷路，除非他們找到出去的唯一一條路。）

♠ **through** 的歷史淵源

through 在古英文中，是用來代表水管通過各地，抵達水龍頭的路徑。承接著一個從「起點」至「終點」的動作，代表「物體與空間的關係，以及該物體的動作與其經過的路徑」。

動詞和介系詞 through 來配對

♠ 談到路徑時，表達穿越（force a way through）的 through

➤ 「pass through 通過、穿越」

Is there any train passing through the dense forests from Himalayas?

（有任何從喜馬拉雅山那頭穿越那座濃密森林的火車嗎？）

➤ 「break through 用蠻力闖進去、闖出去」

The dogs in the fence are trying to break through.

（欄內的狗正在試著逃脫。）

➤ 「cut through 走捷徑」從中間穿越，而不是繞道而行。

The hunter decided to cut through the magic forest.

（獵人決定要穿越魔法森林。）

♠ 維持穿越（force a way through）的概念，語意延伸到其他事務上，例如光的移動軌跡、人生之旅等

➤ 「shines through 灑落」某物灑落在一個立體的空間中。

The sun shines through the dark forest.

（光線灑落陰暗的森林。）

解析

動詞 shine 灑落，表達陽光從「天空」照射到「陰暗的森林」的一個「動作之路徑」，是一個有從「A 點」到「B 點」的位移。

➤ 「live through 經歷某事」

Our grandpa lived through both the World Wars and the Great Depression. He is a centenarian.

（我的爺爺經歷過世界大戰以及經濟大蕭條。他是一位人瑞。）

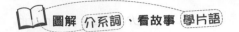

介系詞 through 小學堂

♠ 練習：請選出適當的片語，分別填入下列空白處。

> achieved through
> jumps through hoops
> down through the years
> look through
> through the bottom of

❶ I can sense the heat_____my boots.

❷ My parents are spies! They_____all of my Facebook posts.

❸ The new standards have been_____the integration of the existing ones.

❹ The salesman_____to please every type of customers.

❺ You can't believe how many research papers Dr. Huang published_____.

解答

❶ through the bottom of 從底部傳導。

我可以從我的靴底感受到炎熱。

解析：感受到熱能從地上傳達到腳上。

❷ look through 瀏覽。

我的父母是間諜！他們瀏覽我所有公告在臉書的文章。

❸ achieved through 透過……達成。

新的標準是由現有的標準所整合制訂出來的。

解析：**through** 後面接「達成目的的方法或手段」。

❹ jumps through hoops 跳火圈，為達成目的而經歷苦難或困難，引申為赴湯蹈火。

為了取悅各式各樣的顧客，那位銷售員使出了渾身解數。

❺ down through the years 在一段很長的時間中。

你應該很難相信黃博士在這幾年裡發表了多少篇論文。

around

♠ 談到空間關係時，around 表達「環繞的位置」

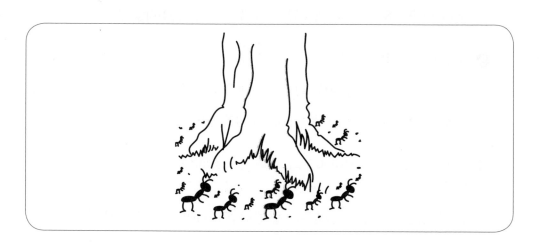

關鍵例句

There are ants around the base of the tree.

（螞蟻圍繞著樹的底部。）

Lisa's friends are sitting around her, celebrating her birthday.

（莉莎的朋友圍坐在她的身旁，慶祝她的生日。）

關於 around 這個介系詞

♠ 談到移動路徑時，around 表達「環繞的路徑」

The boy runs around the baseball field to celebrate the victory.

（男孩環繞棒球場奔跑著慶祝勝利。）

解析

run around 是一個環繞的路徑，不一定是一圈，而是好幾個不規則的小圈，並非直接到達目的地。

Tom hates to go shopping with his girlfriend because she just looks around for a long time without buying anything.

（湯姆不喜歡跟他的女朋友逛街，因為她就是在店內到處看看然後什麼也沒買。）

解析

around 表示「一種沒有目的的環繞路徑」，英文意思為 aimless motion，想像某些女孩子們逛街時，會在店內轉個好幾圈，比較哪一個商品比較好，這就是所謂的 look around，一種隨意看看，沒有一定要購買什麼的逛街方式。

動詞和介系詞 **around** 來配對

♠ 表達路徑迂迴環繞的 around

➤ 「beat around the bush 拐彎抹角」

Please tell the truth. Don't beat around the bush.

（請說實話。別拐彎抹角。）

➤ 「shop around 逛街、貨比三家」

Salesman: This printer is on sale.

Customer: It's beyond my budget.

Salesman: We offer a layaway plan.

Customer: Thank you. I think I will shop around for a better price.

銷售員：這個印表機在特價。

顧客：這超出我預算了。

銷售員：我們提供分期付款的方案。

顧客：謝謝。我打算再逛逛，看有沒有比較好的價錢。

➤ 「turn around 轉頭」

Flora turned around and said goodbye to her parents before the train leaves.

（芙蘿拉在火車開走前，轉頭跟她的父母說再見。）

➤ 「lie around 無所事事」

Son: I don't need education any more.

Mother: Fine! But it doesn't mean you can lie around the house; go get a job at the factory.

Son: Then I will still go to school tomorrow.

兒子：我不想要上學了。

母親：好！但是這並不代表你可以在家裡無所事事，去工廠做工吧。

兒子：那我還是繼續上學好了。

介系詞 around 小學堂

♠ 練習：請選出適當的片語，分別填入下列空白處。

| has been around |
| have been hanging around with |
| revolves around |
| around four o'clock |
| fooling around |

❶ Peter owned a night club and had a good bit of money. It was frustrating because most people in this town left and nobody _____ long enough to remember it.

❷ Dianna and her husband's routine now _____ their weekly visits to the nursing home in New Jersey.

❸ Mom: You _____ Steve a lot. Son: Mom, don't talk to me when I am in the shower. I can't hear you. Mom: I hope you can spend more time studying rather than ❹ _____ with Steve after school every day.Son: We were doing our homework ❺ _____ yesterday. Mom: Did you do homework the day before yesterday? Remember to choose your friends wisely because the company you keep defines you.

解答

❶ has been around 在某處居住一段時間。

彼得開了一間夜店攢了一些錢。但他感到很沮喪，因為大部分的人都離開小鎮了，留著的人們也都不會久留，自然對這個小鎮也沒什麼記憶。

❷ revolves around 將心力專注在某事。

黛安娜與她丈夫現在每週的例行公事就是到紐澤西的養老院拜訪。

解析：雖然 around 是指環繞的路徑，而不是「直接抵達目的地的路」，但與 revolve（旋轉、以某人某事為中心）搭配時，則表示不管旋轉到哪個方向，目的地都圍繞在一個中心點上。

❸ have been hanging around with 最近常跟某人閒混。

❹ fooling around 無所事事地鬼混。
解析：**rather than**（而不是）後面要接名詞片語，例如：動名詞。

❺ around four o'clock 大約四點。

3-5 翻譯：

母親：你最近很常跟史提夫混在一起。

兒子：媽，不要趁我洗澡的時候跟我講話，我聽不到。

母親：我希望你可以多花一些時間讀書，而不是每天下課都跟史提夫鬼混。

兒子：我們昨天四點左右有在做功課喔。

母親：那前天你們有做功課嗎？要慎選朋友呀，你交什麼朋友，你就是怎樣的人。

by

♠ by 談到空間的關係時，by 表示「在……旁邊」，也就是靠近（proximity）的意思。

關鍵例句

Let's sit by the window so we can watch snow falling.

（我們去坐在窗戶旁邊賞雪吧。）

My uncle's house is by the river.

（我叔叔的房子在河流旁邊。）

關於 **by** 這個介系詞

♠ 若談到移動的路徑時，**by** 表示「經過」某物體。

The man goes by the golf course.

（那個男人經過了高爾夫球場。）

動詞和介系詞 **by** 來配對

♠ 表達接近（proximity）的 by

➤ 「stand by 在某人的旁邊」站在某人的旁邊，也引申「支持、陪伴」某人。

Girl: The life is getting tough. I don't know if I can take it anymore.

Boy: Don't worry. I will stand by you.

女孩：生活越來越艱困了，我不知道還能不能承受下去。

男孩：別擔心，我會在你身邊支持你。

➤ 「come by 拜訪」的 by 為「靠近」之意，靠近某人或某人的所在地，也就是拜訪，英文也可表達成 pay a visit。

My client wants me to come by his office tomorrow.

（我的顧客希望我明天可以到他的辦公室拜訪。）

♠ 與「被動語態」連用，表示「動作者的動作」或是
「事件發生的原因」

➤ 「be caused by 由……所造成」

The discrepancy of the twin girls might have been caused by the different ways they are taught at school.

（這對雙胞胎女孩的差異可能是因學校教導方式的不同而造成的。）

➤ 「be surrounded by 被……所圍繞」

Night markets in Taiwan are places surrounded by a variety of street vendors.

（台灣的夜市是個被各式各樣的攤販所圍繞的地方。）

介系詞 **by** 其它應用

♠ 「by the way 順道一提」，提出非原本對話中主要討論的事。by the way 語意延伸自 byway（偏僻小路）。

By the way, you can thank your ex-husband for the hole that's never going to be filled.

（順道一提，你可以謝謝妳的前夫所造成的無法彌補的傷害。）

 介系詞的超級比一比

♠ 比較：表達路徑的 by 與 around。

➤ by 表達從物體的「任一邊經過」

The comet goes by Earth once every 12 years.

（那個彗星每十二年會經過地球一次。）

➤ around 表達以「環繞的方式經過」物體

The man traveled around the world this winter.

（那個男人在今年冬天環遊世界。）

介系詞 by 小學堂

♠ 練習：請選出適當的片語，分別填入下列空白處。

around, by, in, to, for

Allen and Jessie went ❶_____ the same photography class last semester. Jessie was and still is Allen's crush. Allen heard that Jessie goes to Happy Restaurant a lot, so he hangs ❷ _____ the district very often to create a romantic scene like this:

Allen: Hey, Jessie.

Jessie: Hey, Allen. You were ❸ _____ the photography class, weren't you?

Allen: You remembered me. That's sweet.

Jessie: Yeah. I do. What are you here ❹ _____ ?

Allen: Well, I am just passing ❺ _____ . A small city, huh?

解答

❶ to，表達目的地。

❷ around，表示常在那個區域閒晃。

❸ in，表達參加某一個課程。

❹ for，詢問目的。

❺ by，表示只是碰巧經過而已。

翻譯

艾倫與潔西上個學期一起修過攝影課。艾倫從以前到現在都暗戀著潔西。艾倫聽說潔西常去快樂餐館，所以他就常在那個地區晃來晃去想製造類似這樣的浪漫場景：

艾倫：嗨，潔西。

潔西：嗨，艾倫，你也修過攝影課對吧？

艾倫：你記得我，真好。

潔西：對啊。你怎麼會在這呀？

艾倫：嗯……，我只是經過。這個城市真小，對吧？

with

♠ 談到空間關係時，with 表達「近距離」，沒有確定位置的近距離（nonspecific proximity）。

關鍵例句

Boy: Did you see my screw driver?

Girl: Do you mean the small model of Poseidon's trident? It's in the toy box with my Barbie.

Boy: Oh hell no! They are nothing alike.

男孩：你有看到我的螺絲起子嗎？

女孩：你是說波塞頓三叉戟的小模型嗎？在我的玩具盒子中芭比那邊。

男孩：不是吧！他們一點也不像。

解析

with 用來表示螺絲起子跟芭比擺在一起，表示「物體間的鄰近」，但是並「不知道明確位置」。

 關於 **with** 這個介系詞

♠ 用來描述「物品、事物」的「特徵、內容」，其語意也延伸了「鄰近」的意涵

➤ 「a camera with P-iris 有 P-iris 光圈的相機」，使用「名詞＋with＋特徵」表達「有……特色之物品」

Customer: I am looking for a camera with P-iris.

Salesman: You can try this one. It produces images with better clarity and contrast.

解析

新的相機有 P-iris 的光圈，讓相片效果更好，那麼「相機」跟「P-iris 的光圈」兩者都在機身上，是鄰近的關係；而其產生的相片有比較好的色彩清晰度，「相片的影像」與「清晰度、色彩對比」也是鄰近、且有連結的關係。

➤ 「a man with green hair 綠髮男子」 使用「人＋ with ＋顏色＋ hair」表達「有……髮色之人」，with 表示所有物、配件

Did you see the man with green hair?

（你有看到那個綠頭髮的男人嗎？）

動詞和介系詞 with 來配對

♠ 與人溝通、吵架、合作、或各種形式的溝通時，需要人跟人在彼此旁邊

➤ 「discuss with… 與……討論事情」

If you have any comments or problems, feel free to discuss with me.

（如果你有任何意見或問題，隨時跟我討論。）

解析

其他具有思維的交流。或溝通性的動詞都可以跟 with 搭配使用：
communicate with（與 ……溝通）、argue with（與……爭論）、agree with（同意……某事），negotiate with（與……協商），work with（與……合作）。

➤ 「compare A with B 比較 A 與 B 的差別」

Ann will compare the previous report with the current one.

（安會比較舊有報告與目前報告的不同。）

♠ 表達「達成目的」的手段

➤ 「brush the teeth with... 用……來刷牙」，使用「動詞＋with ＋東西」表示藉由「使用某物」來達成目的。

Brush your teeth with the new toothpaste I bought yesterday.

（用我昨天新買的牙膏刷牙吧。）

介系詞的超級比一比

♠ 比較：表達「與……合作的 with」與「為……工作的 for」

I work for Roger. He is an emotional and grumpy boss. Nobody likes to work with him.

（我為羅傑工作，他是一位情緒化又脾氣暴躁的老闆，沒有人喜歡跟他共事。）

解析

❶ A work with B

A 與 B 一起工作，兩個人是合作的關係，且平等的。

❷ A work for B

A 為 B 工作，B 可以對 A 發號司令，職位是不平等的。A 通常是老闆，而 B 是職員。

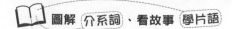

♠ 練習：請選出適當的片語，分別填入下列空白處。

plays badminton with
lives with
consult with
Cut the steak with
deal with

❶ Don't bother your sister. She has some issues to _____.

❷ The girl _____ her high school friend in the rented apartment.

❸ You can _____ the academic advisor about how many courses you should take in your freshman year.

❹ Billy _____ his sister every weekend.

❺ _____ the knife on the table.

解答

❶ deal with 處理棘手的事。

別打擾妳姊姊，她有一些狀況要處理。

解析：處理事情時，需要將心力放在那件事情上，才能處理，是「鄰近、空間意涵」的延伸。

❷ lives with 與……同住。

那位女孩跟她的高中同學一起租房子住。

解析：with 表示陪伴，是實際在彼此身邊，是「鄰近空間意涵」的延伸。

❸ consult with 與……商量、請教。

你可以跟你的學業輔導員商量大一要修多少課程。

❹ plays badminton with 跟……打羽毛球。

比利每個週末都會跟他的妹妹一起打羽毛球。

❺ Cut the steak with... 用……來切牛排。

用桌上的刀子切牛排。

♠ For 表達「目的性」，不像其他介系詞 to、at 表達物體間的空間關係，for 是用來表達目的性的。

關鍵例句

Jessie prayed for forgiveness.

（潔西祈禱能取得原諒。）

解析

Jessie「祈禱」的動作，是為了達到「取得原諒」之目的，介系詞 for，表達「動作」與「目的」間的關係。

When giving others' help, Tim wants for nothing.

（Tim 幫助別人是不求回報的。）

解析

Tim 提供協助時，是「不求回報」（nothing）的，他的目的就是「無所求」。此句透過介系詞 for，表達「動作」與「目的」間的關係。

關於 **for** 這個介系詞

♠ **for 表達某人做某事，是「為了他人的利益著想」。**

The scholar raised money for autism researches.

（那位教授募款是為了自閉症的研究計畫。）

♠ **for 表達「把某物給某人」，for 後面接「受惠者」。**

Tommy bought a diamond ring for his girlfriend.

（湯米買了一個鑽石戒指給他的女友。）

解析

Tommy「購買鑽石」的動作，是為了將此物交給「特定的人」。

介系詞 for 其它應用

♠ 表達目的的 for

➤ 「be available for 可取得的……」

There are hundreds of apps available for your smart watch.

（你的智慧手錶目前有幾百款應用程式可以使用。）

➤ 「be responsible for 為……負責」

Nowadays, public librarians are responsible for providing access to reliable and timely health information.

（現今的圖書館員要負責提供可靠且即時的健康資訊。）

➤ 「yearn / long for 渴望……」

Many city dwellers yearn for a bit of countryside in their balconies.

（很多都市居民渴望能在他們的陽台上注入一些鄉村的氣息。）

Approximately 50% of women having infertility problems have sought medical assistance and are still longing for pregnancy.

（百分之五十不孕症的女性尋求醫療協助，仍然渴望可以懷孕。）

介系詞的超級比一比

♠ 表達「目的」的 to 與 for

當 to 表達「目的時」語意跟 for 類似：

to 表達目的	for 表達目的
動作者的「動作」是達成目的 「直接手段」	動作者的「動作」是達成目的 「間接手段」

請比較兩句：

❶ The man whistled to the life guard.

❷ The man whistled for the life guard.

（那個男人對著救生員吹口哨。）

解析

例句 1：請想像以下情境：假設一個男子在海邊抽筋了，需要救生員的協助，救生員剛好在他的不遠處，他吹了口哨，希望直接引起救生員的注意，這時就要用例句 1。這句的介系詞使用表達「直接手段」的「to」，因為他吹口哨這個動作，直接呼喚到救生員了。

例句 2：一樣的情境下，但是這時候救生員離那男子很遠，男子吹了口哨，希望引起其他遊客的注意，讓其他人幫他呼喚救生員，這時候就要用例句2。這句的介系詞使用表達「間接手段」的「for」，因為他吹口哨這個動作，只是試圖對附近的人呼救，並希望其他人可以幫他呼喚救生員。

PART 1 圖解介系詞篇

PART 2 看故事學片語篇

介系詞 **for** 小學堂

♠ 練習：請選出適當的片語，分別填入下列空白處。

> look for
> pay for
> passion for
> setting off for
> work for

❶ They want us to _____ their mistakes. How ridiculous!

❷ _____ her last destination in the trip, Alice finds out that she doesn't want to go home that early.

❸ Gina has everything you _____ : talent, ability, confidence, and a sense of humor.

❹ The coach sees Fred's potential to be a great basketball player, so he is trying to discover his _____ the sport.

❺ The pill didn't _____ everyone. We are sorry to announce that there is no medicine to cure this disease temporarily.

解答

❶ pay for 付錢、付出代價。

他們要我們為他們的錯誤付出代價，太可笑了！

❷ setting off for 啟程、出發。

前往旅途中最後一站的艾莉絲發現，她並不想這麼早回家。

❸ look for 尋找。

吉娜擁有你所尋找的特質：天賦、能力、自信，以及幽默感。

❹ passion for 對……的熱情。

教練看到佛瑞德有成為一位優秀籃球員的潛力，所以他正在嘗試開發他對於這項運動的熱忱。

❺ work for 對……起作用。work for 一字多義，在其他情境中，可翻譯為「為某人工作」。

這個藥對大家都沒效，我們很抱歉必須宣布暫時沒有任何藥物可以治療這個疾病。

♠ **of 也就是中文的「的」，表達「屬於的關係」。**

➤ 關係 1：「部分與整體」，例如：傑森有很多隻狗，你想表達其中一隻或其中的某些隻時，使用 of，表達全體中的那一個／或多個。

圖 1　over	圖 2　under

關鍵例句

Most of Jason's dogs can swim.

（傑森的狗大部分都會游泳。）

One of Jason's dogs can't swim.

（傑森的其中一隻狗不會游泳。）

➤ 關係 2：「某物的源頭」

The famous black tea is a product of Taiwan.

（那個有名的紅茶是台灣的產品。）

It is a scarf made of silk.

（這是一條絲質的圍巾。）

➤ 關係 3：「人與人、人與團體」或是「人與事件」的關係

Mike is a friend of mine.

（麥可是我的一位朋友。）

They really are a family of geniuses.

（他們一家人真是聰明。）

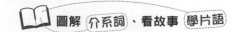

 關於 of 其它應用

♠ Of 也可以作為「同位語」使用

Zac: Is it possible for people gaining <u>1 kilogram of fat</u> in one day?

Rob: Maybe, if you keep eating fatty foods.

柴克：我們真的有可能在一天內增加一公斤的脂肪嗎？

羅伯：如果你一直吃高油脂的食物，有可能喔。

解析

例句中一公斤就是指油脂，兩個名詞呈現互補的關係，讓語意更完完整，即同位語的功能所在。

♠ 其他 of 作為同位語的例子

an increase of 100 pounds

（增加了一百磅）

a decrease of 10%

（減少了百分之十）

♠ 表達源頭的 of

➤「be made of 由 ……製成」表達東西的原料是什麼的 of

The toy is made of plastic.

（這個玩具是用塑膠做的。）

➤ 「come out of 來自於……」

Anya just came out of her mother's womb.

（安雅剛從媽媽的肚子裡蹦出來。）

♠ 表達原因的 of

➤ 「die of 死於 ……」

What a poor man! His son died of starvation, his daughter was sold as a child bride, and his wife was in jail.

（可憐的男人！他的兒子死於飢餓、女兒被賣做童養媳、而妻子在牢裡。）

♠ 做同位語使用的 of

➤ 「think of 這麼想……」

I never thought of that.

（我從來沒那麼想。）

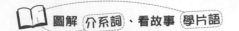

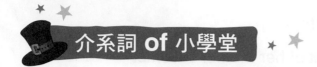 介系詞 of 小學堂

♠ 練習：請選出適當的片語，分別填入下列空白處。

> consist of
> get rid of
> one of a kind
> Speak of the devil
> part of

❶ What does a balanced diet _____ ?

❷ A variety of vegetables supply essential vitamins and minerals to meet your body's needs, so the intake of vegetables is an important _____ a healthy diet.

❸ To most people, my wife would be arrogant. But to me, she is amusing and endearing. She is _____ .

❹ The angry daughter yelled at her father: "So now you want to _____ me because I am useless, is that it?"

❺ _____ and he will come.

解答

❶ consist of 由……組成。

均衡的飲食需要包含什麼？

❷ part of 為……的一部分。

各種蔬菜可以提供身體必須的維他命與礦物質，以符合身體對營養的需求，所以蔬菜的攝取是健康飲食重要的一環。

❸ one of a kind 獨一無二的。

對大多數人來說，我太太可能顯得傲慢，但對我來說，她好笑又可愛，是獨一無二的。

❹ get rid of 擺脫某人。

憤怒的女兒對著她的父親大喊：「所以現在你想要擺脫我因為我很沒用，是這樣嗎？」

❺ Speak of the devil 說曹操曹操就到。

Prepositions of Time

♠ 表達時間的介系詞（Prepositions of Time）：表達時間，介系詞是很重要的角色，本單元統一將表達時間的介系詞統整如下：

關鍵例句

❶ In the 18th century, the signal of wealth is how much land people own.

（十八世紀的時候，財富的象徵是一個人所擁有的土地。）

❷ Megan was born on December 25, 2009.

（梅根在 2009 年 12 月 25 日出生。）

❸ She got married at the age of 15.

（她十五歲就結婚了。）

解析

　　in、on、at 所表達的時間點的差異在於 in 代表較為籠統的時間，而 at 則是較為明確的時間； on 則位於兩者中間。下表以「時間明確性」的程度來呈現：

大致上、籠統的時間明確、具體的時間		
（general）————————➤（specific）		
in	on	at
in the morning 在早晨	on Monday 星期一	at 6:45 六點四十五分
in time 及時	on November, 2016 2016 年的 11 月	at dawn（註 1） 黎明時
in August 在八月	on Christmas Day 在聖誕節晚上	at Easter time（註 2） 在復活節期間
in 1988 在 1988 年	on his birthday 在他的生日	at the end of the month 月底

註 1 dawn 指破曉時分，也就是太陽乍現的時刻。

註 2 當你要表達節慶的時間，則使用「at＋節慶名稱」；若是指節慶當天，則用「on＋節慶名稱＋day」。

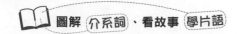

♠ 表達在不超過某個時間點的 by

John has to submit the report by 9 P.M.

（強尼必須要在晚上九點前交出報告。）

> 註 by 表達時間時，英文意思為 no later than（不能晚於這個時間）

♠ 表達在某個時間點先後的 around/ about

The accident happened around 4 o'clock.

（那場意外發生在四點左右。）

介系詞的超級比一比

♠ 表達「一段明確時間」的介系詞

The professor's office hour is between 3 and 4 o'clock.

（那位教授的晤談時間是在三點到四點之間。）

Madeline teaches dance from 7 to 9 every Friday evening.

（瑪德琳每週五晚上七點到九點教舞。）

♠ 表達從開始至終的 through

Maggie takes care of grandmother all through the night.

（瑪姬照顧奶奶一整晚。）

♠ 表達一段時間的 for

The immigrant population has remained stable for 3 years.

（移民的人口數三年來都處於穩定。）

This is an important breakthrough for now.

（以現在來說，這是很重要的突破了。）

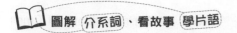

介系詞 from、by、in、on、at 小學堂

♠ 練習：請選出適當的片語，分別填入下列空白處。

> from　by　on　in　at

❶ The manager wants you to finish it ＿＿＿＿＿ Monday.

❷ The train left ＿＿＿＿＿ 5:30.

❸ He met his wife in an Irish bar ＿＿＿＿＿ the 1990s.

❹ They planned to visit their grandparents ＿＿＿＿＿ New Year's Eve.

❺ Daily Brunch opens ＿＿＿＿＿ 8:00 to 20:00 everyday.

解答

❶ by。

經理希望你可以在星期一前完成。

❷ at。

火車五點三十分離開。

❸ in。

他在九零年代一間愛爾蘭酒吧遇見他的太太。

❹ on。

他們計畫在除夕拜訪爺爺奶奶。

❺ from。

天天早午餐每天從早上八點開到晚上十點。

PART 2
看故事學片語篇

unit 01

Dating Mark
和馬可交往

 片語搶先看

1. to stop... from 阻止	2. to take exercise 運動
3. call up 打電話	4. lie down 躺下
5. to look at 注視	6. to tired out 非常疲倦
7. little by little 逐漸地	

 **看日記學英文**

I have been dating Mark for over six months. My first impression of him is a very positive boy who is self-disciplined in managing his health and figure. I just thought he is that kind of person who pushes himself hard. I didn't notice that he is addicted to taking exercise. I mean he is that kind of guy who would spend hours at the gym. The only time I successfully stopped him from working out was on my birthday. He became depressed and easily irritated the other day. It's definitely a kind of behavioral addition which I can't do anything about it. Taking exercise regularly is no doubt good for health. I do agree. But it's way too much that we as a couple can't go out on a date like normal people, and even sometimes, we can't rely on each other for help. One day I called him up when an emergence occurred; he missed my calls for like twenty times. Tonight, lying down on my bed, I look at the picture of Mark and me. Something just doesn't feel right. The whole thing has tired me out little by little.

　　我已經跟馬可交往六個月了，我記得對他的第一印象是個很正向，對於自我健康管理很嚴謹的男生。我一開始以為他只是對自己很嚴格罷了，我並沒有注意到，他對運動上癮，我是指是那種一天花數小時在健身房的人，之前我有一次，也是唯一一次，成功讓他為了我的生日而不去健身房，但是隔天他變得很低落並且易怒，這根本是一種行為成癮，而我也不能做什麼。我的確認同規律的運動對健康很好，但是他真的太超過了，導致我們無法像正常情侶一樣出去約會，我們甚至還不能互相幫忙。有一次我因為突然有緊急狀況，所以打了二十幾通電話給他，他卻一通也沒接到。今晚我躺在床上，看著我跟馬可的照片，覺得事情不對勁，這整件事情一點一點的把我擊敗。

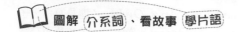

 片語有道理

中文意思天差地別，但是在英文中，字形卻非常相似，而在時態的變化上更容易讓人混淆，請見下表：

	現在式	現在分詞	過去式	過去分詞
說謊	lie	lying	lied	lied
躺	lie	lying	lay	lain
放著	lay	laying	laid	laid

要區分以上三個字，説謊 lie 的意思比較容易區隔，而躺 lie 以及放著 lay 由於都是物理上將身體放下，或是將物品放下的動作，其中的差別為：

> lie 躺著，英文意思為 to put oneself in a horizontal position 即平躺之意。躺在某某地方，表達休息之意的片語：「lie down＋表位置、目的等地介系詞＋地點」。

❶ Mark lies down on the couch at once as soon as he gets home from work.

（馬可一下班回家，會立刻躺在沙發上。）

❷ Many homeless people sought a shelter beneath an overpass and lay down on the ground.

（很多無家可歸的人在高架橋下找遮蔽，並且直接躺在地上。）

❸ Let the injured lie down for a rest.

（讓受傷的人躺下來休息。）

> 註　lie down 為不及物動詞片語，必須先接介系詞後，才能直接加上
> 受詞，例如：lie down on the grass 在草地上躺著。

> lay 放置，英文意思為 to put something in a particular place，即放下、放著之意。將某東西放置在某某地方：「lay＋東西 ／ 事件＋down＋（in ／ on＋something）」。

❶ My boyfriend says that I can lay my worries down and stay with him.

（我男朋友説我可以跟著他，甚麼都不用擔心（放下擔心）。）

❷ Mia laid a dog on the table.

（米亞把狗狗放在桌上。）

> 註　lay 為及物動詞，後須接受詞，例如：lay the basket down 把籃
> 子放下。另外，可能你會也聽到 get laid 的這種用法，get laid
> 表達與某人發生關係之意，常見的情境是你的好姊妹關心你昨
> 晚跟心儀對象約會的進度，這時她可以那麼問你：
>
> Did you get laid last night?
>
> （你昨晚發生關係了嗎？）

♠ stop 終止、stop 阻止

• 當你想表達某件事情停止了：**stop** 終止，英文意思為 *not continue*，即某件事情不再持續。

The rain stopped. Let's go for mountain climbing.

（現在雨停了，我們去爬山吧。）

> 註 「stop ＋V-ing」表示某件過去持續發生的事件終止了。

• 當你想表達 **A** 阻止 **B** 的概念：**stop** 阻止，英文意思為 *prevent*，即不讓某事件發生之意。表達阻止某件事情之發生：「*stop*＋某件事情（受詞）」

❶ "No smoking policy" is used to stop air pollution from happening.

（「不抽菸政策」是用來防止空氣污染的發生。）

❷ I know that nothing can stop you from quitting the high-paying job.

（我知道沒有任何事可以阻止你把那個好工作辭掉。）

- 表達阻止某件事情發生，並強調該事件不該往某個方向走：

  「stop＋某件事情／某件事情（受詞）＋ from＋動詞」

  Leo tries to stop his voice from trembling.

  （里奧試著不要讓他的聲音顫抖。）

Memories With Mark
與馬可相處的時光

 片語搶先看

1. look for 尋找	2. take a look at 看一看
3. all right 沒關係	4. look at 看著
5. would like to 想要	6. take out 帶某人出去約會
7. have a good time 　過得愉快	

 看對話學英文

Eva recalled those good times she and Mark had together. It was a rainy Sunday when most of the people went shopping. The furniture warehouses were packed with people. Eva was there, feeling eager to find a new mattress to replace her old one, which made her wake up tired and achy all over the body. She approached to a salesperson for help.

伊娃回想起與馬可相處的時光。那是一個下雨的週日午後，大部分的人

都跑去購物了。家具行充滿了人，伊娃也在其中，想要找到一個新的床墊去替換舊的，那個讓她每天起床又累又酸痛的東西。她上前詢問銷售員尋求協助。

E ▶ Eva 伊娃　**S** ▶ Salesperson 銷售員　**M** ▶ Man 男人

E I am looking for a plush mattress. Is there any item on sale? My old one is driving me crazy. (She scratched her back while talking.)

（我在找一張軟床墊，有優惠的款式嗎？我家的那個要把我逼瘋了。（邊說邊抓背））。

S Ahh, bed bugs issues. (The salesperson murmured.) Please follow me. Please take a look at this one. It is the best seller with 90% of customer satisfaction.

（噢，看來是床蝨問題（說得非常小聲），請跟我來，請看看這一款，這是我們的熱銷款，百分之 90 的顧客也很滿意。）

While Eva was lying down on the mattress, there came a man trying to lie down and experience the mattress as well.

當艾娃在試躺時，一個男人也突然躺上來。

E It feels soft... Ouch.

（感覺很柔軟……啊！）

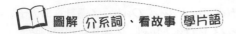

Ⓜ I am so sorry.

（我很抱歉。）

Ⓔ It's all right.

（沒關係。）

The man looked at her as if they had met before.

男人看著伊娃，好像他們以前認識一樣。

Ⓔ Don't stare at me. I'm fine.

（別盯著我看，我沒事。）

Ⓜ My name is Mark. I would like to take you out for dinner to show my apology.

（我的名字是馬可，我想帶你吃個晚餐，當作賠禮。）

Ⓔ Well..., that could be nice.

（嗯……，好啊。）

On that rainy afternoon, both of them had a good time.

那天下雨的午後，兩個人都過得很愉快。

片語有道理

當你想要表達想要、未來的想法，或夢想時，可用以下的方式表達：

> **want to** 想要、**hope to** 想要、**would like to** 想要。以上的片語均可以互相替換，但是當你想委婉地表達想要的時候，**want to** 的情感比較直接，而 **would like to** 則比較有禮貌：

❶ Amy is bossy. When she says she <u>wants something, she wants to have them</u> at once.

（艾咪喜歡頤指氣使。當她說她想要什麼時，她立刻就想要擁有。）

❷ Eva says <u>she would like</u> to move in and live with me.

（伊娃說她想要搬進來跟我一起住。）

> 以下的片語均須搭配不定詞用法，片語後需要加動詞：

❶ I want to <u>help people</u>.

（我想要幫助人。）

❷ I hope to <u>be a missionary</u>.

（我想成為傳教士。）

❸ I would like to <u>serve God</u>.

（我想要為上帝做事。）

當你要表達不想要、不願意時，則加入否定詞：

❶ I don't want to help people.

（我不想要幫助人。）

❷ I never hope to be a missionary.

（我從來不曾想要成為一位傳教士。）

❸ I wouldn't like to serve God.

（我不願意為上帝服務。）

當你詢問別人想不想吃東西、想不想喝飲料時，可以使用
「**Would you like**＋食物名稱」：

A: Would you like some milk?

（需要一些牛奶嗎？）

B: Yes, I'd like some.

（好的，我要一些。）

一字多義

♠ take 拿出；帶某人出去；外帶

♠ **take** 為動詞時，有拿、取之意，而搭配介系詞 out，可表達拿出、外帶、帶某人出去之意。

- **take out 拿出**

Mark takes out his wallet to pay the bill.

（馬可拿出他的皮包付帳。）

- **take something out 把東西拿出來**

Mark is such a decent guy. He takes his handkerchief out to wipe my tears during the movie.

（馬可真是個紳士。看電影的時候，他把他的手帕拿出來幫我擦眼淚。）

- **take somebody out 邀約某人去看電影、吃飯**

Mark took me out for a movie.

（馬可帶我去看電影。）

- **takeout/ takeaway 外帶的食物，為名詞。**

Let's have a takeout tonight.

（我們今晚叫外賣吧。）

Can't Help Being Addicted To Him
深深被馬可吸引

片語搶先看

1. end up 結果是	2. at the same time 同時
3. arrive at 到達	4. make fun of 取笑
5. be full of 充滿	6. in vain 徒勞無功
7. base on 根據	

看日記學英文

To avoid the annoying heat from the sun, Mark and I ended up having the dinner at a self-serve ice cream shop. We arrived at the shop around noon, and it is full of people. People all lined up for ice cream machines, so we had to wait for a while. Aside from the long wait, it was fun to learn about him based on his topping choices. He gave himself a nick name of Mr. Gummy Bear. At the same time, I was called the Healthy

Nuts Lady. We made fun of each other. He seems to be an open-minded person, but once the conversation was directed to what we do for living, his face turned stern for a second, then he hid his emotion. Later on, a witty humor came from his lip, "I live to give and give to live. It's an ancient Indian secret." I tried to dig for more answers but was in vain. While I was wondering if this guy has trouble getting close to people, I was so drawn by him that I told him everything about me. He just had the magic to make me trust him.

為了要遠離日曬與炎熱，馬可與我的道歉晚餐結果改在一間自助冰淇淋店。我們大約中午抵達，店裡充滿了排隊等冰淇淋機的人，所以我們等了一下子。雖然我們等蠻久的，但從他的冰淇淋配料選擇，了解他是什麼樣的人是很有趣的事，他自稱他自己是小熊軟糖先生，而我則被取了個養生核果小姐的綽號，我們彼此開著玩笑。他似乎是個心胸開放的人，但是我們的話題只要一轉到職涯生活，他的臉就變得嚴厲，又瞬間收回情緒，後來他嘴角露出機智詼諧的一笑，說：「我們人類活著是為奉獻，並為奉獻而活著，古印度的智慧是這麼告訴我的。」後來我試著挖掘這方面的答案，但都沒有成功，而當我在想這個男人是不是無法打開心房接近他人時，我自己卻深受他吸引，將自己的事情都告訴他了，他真的就有那種讓人信任的魔力。

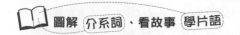

 片語有道理

用形容詞 full、packed、crowded 來表達某個空間充滿人：

> 當你要表達人很多時，用 **full** 充滿的

The museum <u>is full of</u> tourists.

（博物館充滿觀光客。）

> 當你要表達某個空間的人太多了，人滿為患時，用
> **packed** 塞得滿滿的、**crowded** 擁擠的

❶ a <u>packed</u> museum

（充滿人潮的博物館）

❷ The museum <u>is packed with</u> people on weekends.

（那博物館在週末都人潮洶湧。）

❸ a <u>crowded</u> mall

（擁擠的購物中心）

❹ The mall that is on annual sale <u>is crowded with</u> shoppers.

（周年慶的購物中心充滿了購物人潮。）

用動詞 *pack* 來表達人潮擁擠。*pack* 單詞的意思為打包行李、塞滿（東西）、擠滿（人）。*pack* 作擁擠時，英文意思為 *full of people or having too many people*，也就是擠滿人的意思。

People from all over the world <u>packed</u> Time Square to celebrate the New Year.

（世界各地的人們聚集在紐約時報廣場慶祝新年。）

一字多義

♠ 根據 is based on、according to

♠ 雖然 base on 與 according to 的中文翻譯語意相似，但很容易搞混兩者的用法。

- **base on** 以……為基礎。base 單詞意思為 foundation（基礎），思想上的發想點，例如：當醫生在診斷病人時，病人過去的病史是醫師開處方籤的依據，病人對特定的藥物過敏會影響醫生開藥的決定，又例如：常有作家的作品是依據自己的童年為出發點來發揮的，那麼不同作家所經歷的童年不同，而由於基準點不同，其所寫的故事也不相同。

❶ The diagnosis the doctor made <u>is based on</u> the patient's history.

（這位醫生根據病人的病歷來做診斷。）

❷ The story of the bestseller <u>was based on</u> the author's family history.

（這本暢銷書的故事是根據作者的家族故事來改編的。）

- **according to** 根據。*accord* 單詞意思為 *agreement*（一致、協定），用來表達兩個事件的一致性、相同性，例如：下屬必須根據上司的指令來執行任務，其中下屬的執行方式與上司的期待要有一致性；科學家的理論發表必須以實驗的結果為基礎，而理論與實驗的結果必須要有一致性，前後呼應。

❶ Peter installed the software <u>according to</u> the instructions on the user's manual.

（彼得依照使用者手冊的指示安裝軟體。）

❷ <u>According to</u> the annual report, the company reduced greenhouse gas by 2.7 % in 2014.

（根據年報，這間公司的的溫室氣體在 2014 年時減少了百分之 2.7。）

unit 04

Girls' Talk
好姐妹聊心事

 片語搶先看

1. much to one's relief 令人鬆一口氣	2. act out 表現得像在演戲一樣
3. have a date with 與某人約會	4. in no way 絕不是
5. fall head over heels in love with 瘋狂的愛上某人	6. fall in love with 愛上某人
7. get along with 與某人相處愉快	

 看對話學英文

When Eva was looking for an apartment to rent on Fillmore Street last year, she met Renee, a girl who looks young, but acts quite rational. They were strangers then, and now they have become friends and roommates.

當伊娃去年在費爾摩街找出租公寓時，她遇見了芮妮，她看起來年紀很小可是行事上卻很理性。她們那個時候還是陌生人，但是現在卻成為室友外加閨蜜。

E ▶ Eva 伊娃　　　　**R** ▶ Rene 芮妮

R Much to my relief, my innocent and naive girl gets home safely.

（我家無辜的女孩安全回家了，我真是鬆了一口氣。）

E Stop acting out. I was just having a date with a guy.

（別再演了，我只不過出去約個會而已。）

R Yeah, a stranger you met on a mattress. How romantic.

（喔是啊，一個你在床墊上遇到的男人嘛，真浪漫。）

E Be as ironic as you like. You worry too much. I am an adult. Don't forget that I am technically three years older than you. Older and more mature.

（你要怎麼嘲弄我都可以，你太操煩了，我已經是成年人了，而且技術上來說，我的實際年齡比你大三歲，比你年長成熟。）

R Literally yes that you are older. But you are in no way more mature.

（字面上來說你的確比較老，但是你可是一點也不成熟喔。）

E Anyway. I think I am falling head over heels in love with Mark.

159

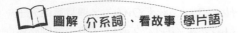

（不跟妳爭了。我覺得我好像瘋狂愛上馬可了。）

R That's not unusual. You can easily fall in love with some guy you met in the bar. And the feeling fades away within a week.

（這一點也不稀奇，你對於酒吧遇到的男人都可以輕易愛上，然後這種愛的感覺在一週內就會慢慢消失。）

E He thinks the same way as I do. He said that he looks forward to seeing me, soon, very soon.

（他跟我有相同的感受，他說他期待很快再見到我，很快就會了。）

R That's what men said to be nice and polite- a basic rule when guys want to get intimated.

（男人都會這樣說以表示友善及禮貌，這是他們想接近女人的基本原則。）

E No, it's more than that. We do get along well, and we feel a strong connection between each other.

（不，不是這樣的，絕對不僅如此，我們不僅相處得宜，還對彼此有強烈的連結感。）

片語有道理

當你想要表達心中釋懷、驚訝、後悔的情緒時，可使用 relief（釋懷）、surprise（詫異）、regret（後悔）：

> **relief** 慰藉、緩和。英文意思為 remove of pain, grief, distress, sickness，表達心中的痛苦、感傷、壓力、疾病的解除。

> **surprise** 驚訝、詫異。英文意思為 to be astonished because of something unexpected，表達因為超乎預期的事情而感到驚訝。

> **regret** 後悔、惋惜。英文意思為 to feel sorrowful when looking back on something you did，表達因為過去的事情而感到傷心，心中有種失去什麼的傷感。

使用下列的片語來表達你對某件事情的感受：

> **to my relief** 表示心情的放鬆、安心、釋懷之意、**to her surprise / astonishment** 表示驚訝、震驚、**to his regret** 表示後悔。接在後面的句子所呈現的事件，必須對應說話者對事件的反應：

❶ <u>To Ally's surprise</u>, she went home and found her husband in the kitchen cooking dinner.

（令艾莉驚訝的是，她一回家就看到丈夫在廚房煮菜。）

❷ <u>Much to John's regret</u>, he never cooks for his beloved wife.

（令約翰感到後悔的是，他從來沒有為自己心愛的太太煮飯。）

❸ <u>To Ally's great relief</u>, her husband finally understands her decision and make sacrifices.

（令艾莉釋懷的事，她的丈夫終於理解她的決定，並做一些犧牲。）

愛上某人的幾種說法：

John 重新回想當初與太太 Ally 的初識場景，並運用下列片語：
★ catch one's eye 吸引某人目光
★ have a crush on someone 對某人心動了
★ fall for someone 愛上某人
★ fall in love with someone 愛上某人
★ fall head over heels for/with someone 對某人深深陷入愛戀

❶ Among the packed fans in front of the stage, the beautiful girl <u>caught my eye</u>.

（舞台前的眾多粉絲中，一位美麗的女孩吸引我的目光。）

❷ She is Ally; I <u>fell for her</u> within only ten minutes.

（她就是艾莉，我在十分鐘之內就愛上她了。）

❸ I told my friend that I finally met a girl whom <u>I have a crush on</u>.

（我告訴我的朋友我終於碰到讓我心動的女孩了。）

❹ I knew this time is different. I not only <u>fall in love with</u> her but fall head over heels for her.

（我知道這次是不同的，我不僅是愛上她，我是深深地愛上她。）

Work! Work! Work!
工作！工作！工作！

 ## 片語搶先看

1. try ones' best 盡力做到最好	2. all at once 立即、馬上
3. sold out 賣光了	4. in a wink of an eye 立即、馬上
5. tear down 拆下	6. put up 建造

 看對話學英文

Eva is now a licensed real estate agent. Her first client is Barbara who works at M & S, a multinational retail-clothing company. As a secretary to CEO, Barbara tries her best to find a new factory in Taiwan for her boss to sell new products.

伊娃現在是一位具有證照的房地產經紀人，她的第一位客戶是芭芭拉，她在一間跨國的服裝零售公司工作。身為總裁秘書，芭芭拉努力地為她

的老闆在台灣找到一間新的工廠,以銷售新的產品。

E ▶ Eva 伊娃   **B** ▶ Barbara 芭芭拉

B The developing community is not a very ideal choice.

(開發中的社區不太理想。)

E I understand your concern. I got a new property for sale all at once this morning.

(我理解你的考量。我今天早上才臨時接到一個新的房地產要賣。)

Eva shows Barbara a document.

伊娃把一份文件給芭芭拉看。

E It is a well-maintained hat manufactory, located in the industrial park. Would you like to visit the factory this afternoon?

(這是一間狀況良好的帽子工廠,位於工業園區。今天下午有興趣去參觀嗎?)

B Of course. It sounds like an unusual chance.

(當然,這聽起來是個難得的機會。)

E You made a good decision. Some of the property sold out just in a wink of an eye.

(這是個正確的決定,有些房地產在一眨眼的時間就賣掉了。)

B You are so right. When I saw an ideal property, I can't decide if I want to take it or not. I have to wait for my boss's approval.

（你說的沒錯。我看到理想的房子時，我無法決定要不要，我得等老闆的決定。）

E Somebody takes it while you are waiting for approval.

（然後當你在等待裁示的時候，房子就被買走了。）

B You tell me.

（就是這樣。）

E If your boss wants to develop hat product lines, this factory would be a good choice. You don't have to tear down anything to put up a new one.

（如果你的老闆想要發展帽子這項產品，這間工廠是個不錯的選擇。你不用拆掉任何東西去蓋新的。）

Ep 1：Meeting the One and Only ／遇見真命天子
Unit 5 Work! Work! Work! ／工作！工作！工作！

PART 1 圖解介系詞篇

PART 2 看故事學片語篇

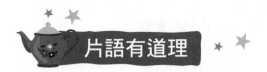

片語有道理

在商場上常常會看到關於商品狀態的標語：

new 新產品

on sale 特賣中

upcoming 即將推出

sold out 售罄

out of stock 目前沒有貨

> 要表達東西賣光了時：*sell out* 賣完了。由於賣完這個動作是在客戶詢問之前就已經發生了，使用過去式。

The new cameras featuring with varifocal lens <u>sold out</u>.

（有變焦鏡頭的新型相機已經賣完了。）

> *be sold out* 被搶購一空。使用被動式來描述商品賣完的狀態，若要強調該產品處於銷售一空的狀態，除了顯示出商品受歡迎之程度，還能告知買家，目前是沒有貨的狀態，使用現在式：

The upcoming concert tickets <u>are fully sold out</u>.

（那個演唱會的門票已經銷售一空了。）

以形容詞表達某項商品賣完了：*sold out* 賣完

The football tickets are <u>sold out</u> within hours.

（足球票在幾小時內賣完了。）

以名詞表達某項商品賣完了：*sell-out* 賣完

The India tour package is a <u>sell-out</u>.

（印度的旅遊行程都全數售完。）

 一字多義

♠ tear down 拆毀、tear apart 撕裂、in tears 哭泣貌

• **tear down** 拆毀，將建築物拆掉。英文意思為 *to pull down a construction such as buildings or walls*。

The government decides to <u>tear down</u> the old station.

（政府決定將舊的車站拆除。）

• **tear apart** 撕裂，將東西撕裂成兩半。英文意思為 *to pull something into pieces*。

Vito <u>tore his son's report card apart</u>.

（維多把他兒子的成績單撕裂。）

Ep 1 : Meeting the One and Only ／遇見真命天子
Unit 5 Work! Work! Work! ／工作！工作！工作！

PART 1 圖解介系詞篇

PART 2 看故事學片語篇

- **in tears** 哭泣貌，梨花帶淚的樣子。英文意思為 *to cry with liquid dropping from the eyes*。

Little Willy yells at his father <u>in tears</u>.

（小威利哭著對他的爸爸大吼。）

Thinking Of Mark All The Time
魂不守舍

片語搶先看

1. look at 看著	2. watch ones' step 小心
3. fall to the ground 跌倒	4. in time 在某截止時間之內／及時
5. come to one's aid 前來援助某人	6. no big deal 沒事的、不麻煩

看對話學英文

Barbara and her boss, Mr. Cooper, made an appointment with Eve to come to the factory for the evaluation. Eva waits for their coming in front of the building. At the end of the street comes a white convertible. The car stops right at the factory;a tall man comes out of it. Eva looked at him with astonishment.

芭芭拉和他的老闆庫伯先生和伊娃約好時間到工廠來做評估。伊娃在工

廠前面等待他們的到來，街尾出現了一台白色的敞篷車，就停在工廠前，一位高大的男子走出來，伊娃看震驚地看著他。

E ▶ Eva 伊娃　**B** ▶ Barbara 芭芭拉　**C** ▶ Mr. Cooper 庫柏先生

B This is Mr. Cooper. This is Miss Griffin, the real estate agent representing the owner of the property.

（這位是庫伯先生，這位是格里芬小姐，她是房地產經紀人，代表這間工廠的老闆出售資產。）

E Mark?

（馬可？）

B Do you know each other?

（你們認識彼此嗎？）

Mr. Cooper ignores his secretary's question.

庫伯先生忽略了他秘書的問題。

C It's nice meeting you, Miss Griffin.

（很高興認識你，格里芬小姐。）

They walk into the factory for a tour.

他們走進了工廠。

E This building includes an office area on the left corner, a warehouse for yarns, and a sewing room for product lines.

（這棟建築物包括了左方角落的辦公區域、儲存毛線的倉庫，以及生產的車間。）

The aisles are packed with bags of colorful knitting samples. It's hard for Eva to introduce the layout of the factory and watch her step at the same time.

走道間充滿了一袋袋彩色的針織樣品，對伊娃來說很難同時介紹工廠的空間規劃並好好地走路。

E Ouch!

（啊！）

Eva falls to the ground. Mr. Cooper catches her from falling just in time.

伊娃跌倒在地，庫伯先生即時扶住她。

C Be careful.

（小心點。）

E Thank you for coming to my aid, Mark.

（謝謝你來扶我，馬可。）

B Are you all right?

（你沒事吧。）

E No big deal. Shall we move to the warehouse?

（沒事。我們要往倉庫看看嗎？）

 片語有道理

表達跌倒、滑倒、失足各式各樣的糗樣時：fall v. 跌倒。英文意思為 come suddenly to the ground，表示由於身體不穩而撞到地上的狀況。

fall 可以當作不及物動詞，不需要加受詞：

Nat stumbled over a stone and <u>fell</u>.

（奈特被石頭絆住就跌倒了。）

fall 也可以當作及物動詞，後面加上介系詞片語表達跌倒的方向。

Nat went horse riding only once in his life because he used to <u>fall from horse back</u> and hurt his legs.

（奈特一生只騎過一次馬，因為他曾經從馬背上摔下來並傷了腿。）

跌倒的原因有很多種，常見的原因是絆到石頭等物品或是滑倒：因絆到腳而身體不穩的說法有：*stumble over* 絆倒、*trip over* 絆倒

❶ Harry <u>stumbles over</u> the staircase and falls on his way to the MRT station.

（哈利在趕去捷運車站時，在樓梯上絆倒了。）

❷ The robber <u>tripped over</u> a stone on the street and got caught by the police.

（那個強盜在路上被石頭絆倒了，並且被警察抓住。）

> 因為路面滑而摔倒：**slip over** 滑倒。英文意思為 *lose your footing and slide for a short distance*，表達原本規律的腳步受到干擾而跌落在地，向前滑行一小段距離的狀況。

Joy <u>slipped over on the ice and fell</u> while she was ice-skating with her boyfriend.

（當喬在跟男友溜冰的時候，滑倒在冰上了。）

♠ see 看見、look at 看著、watch a movie 看電影

- **see** 看見。*see* 表達一種視覺能力，例如你非常害怕血，可是當你走在路上突然有車禍發生時，你無法決定自己要不要看到血，若事件發生在你的視覺範圍內，你就會看到。

I <u>saw</u> a terrible car accident on the street.

（我在路上看到一個可怕的車禍。）

- **look at 看著**。*look at* 表達縮小視野並專注你的視力於某處的狀態，當你走在路上看到特別的咖啡店，想叫你的朋友看看時，就可以這麼說。

Look at the restaurant next to the post office! It is so delicate.

（你看郵局旁邊的餐廳，好別緻喔。）

- **watch 看、觀賞**。*watch* 表達你用眼睛長時間觀賞某部電影、藝術品或值得欣賞的事物。

Watching movies is a popular leisure activity for young people.

（對年輕人來說，看電影是常見的休閒活動。）

He Is Really Into Me.
他真的很愛我

 片語搶先看

1. roll down 滑下	2. get in 進去
3. give in 讓步	4. used to 過去常常
5. turn into 轉變成	6. feel flattered 覺得被諂媚了
7. into somebody 喜歡某人	

 **看對話學英文**

When Eva gets out of her office, she spots a familiar white car. To her surprise, the man rolling the windows down is Mark. He waves to Eva, and Eva walks toward him.

當伊娃走出她的辦公室時,他看到一台熟悉的白色跑車,令她驚訝的是,搖下車窗的人竟然是馬可。他向她揮手,伊娃也走向他。

E ▶ Eva 伊娃 　　　**M** ▶ Mark 馬可

E Mark, you owe me an explanation!

（馬可，你欠我一個解釋。）

M So here I am. Let me take you to dinner.

（所以我來了，我帶你去吃晚餐吧。）

E I have to submit a report no later than tomorrow morning.

（我有一個報告明天早上以前要交。）

M But you have to eat. Get in the car.

（但你總要吃東西吧，上車吧。）

Eva gives in. She feels comfortable with his being overprotective.

伊娃屈服了，她喜歡他過度保護的態度。

M How was your day?

（今天過得好嗎？）

E It was good, Mr. Copper.

（很好，庫伯先生。）

M Call me Mark. What do you want for dinner? I know a nice Thai food restaurant here and I used to go that restaurant often.

（叫我馬可吧。晚餐想吃什麼呢？我知道一家不錯的泰式餐廳，我以前很常去。）

E I hate spicy food.

（我討厭辣的東西。）

Mark looks into Eva's eyes affectionately when they stop for traffic light.

當他們在等紅綠燈時，馬可深情的看著伊娃。

M How about me? I taste sweet, not spicy.

（那我呢？我吃起來是甜甜的，一點也不辣。）

Eva smiles and it turns into laughter. Although the joke is not funny at all, she feels flattered.

伊娃笑了又爆笑出聲，雖然這個笑話一點也不好笑，但是她覺得滿足。

M Let's go to the restaurant you like.

（我們就去你喜歡的餐廳吧。）

What Eva knows for sure is that this guy is really into her. He not only likes to spend time with her, but also loves to give her what she wants.

伊娃可以確定的是這個男人是真的喜歡她的，他不僅喜歡花時間跟她在一起，也願意給她想要的東西。

片語有道理

不管是在戀愛中還是各種人際關係的相處，兩個人以上的相處都會遇到要決定事情的時候，若意見不合，則需要一方妥協或讓步，表示妥協的英文片語有：

> *give in* 投降，表示完全讓步。

Thomas is very stubborn. He doesn't know the meaning of giving in, and he never makes compromises.

（湯馬士非常固執，他不知道投降是什麼，也從來不退讓。）

> *make compromises* 妥協，表示部分讓步。

Thomas believes his new girlfriend, Jamie, is that kind of girl who makes compromises. He likes girls who obey.

（湯馬士相信他的新女友潔咪，是那種會退讓的女孩。他喜歡服從的女人。）

> *meet somebody halfway* 取中間值，表部分讓步。

Jamie tries to make Thomas meet her halfway but is in vain.

（潔咪試著要讓湯馬士對她讓步，但總是失敗。）

註 compromise 這個字是由 com＋promise 所組成的，com 這個字

根代表「一起」的意思，也就是英文的 together；而 promise 為承諾的意思；compromise 可以想成兩個人一起的決定，英文意思為 mutual agreement or a mutual promise made between two or more people。而由於每個人都是一個有思想的個體，兩個人或多人一起做的決定，就是有人會做出讓步的決定，也就是妥協。

 一字多義

♠ get in 進去、get in 被錄取、get in 抵達

in 可以表達在某範圍之內（within），或是進入到某個範圍中（inside），get in 則可以表達進入到某個範圍中，延伸出「進去」、「取得錄取資格」、「抵達」的意思。

- **get in** 進入、進入到某個範圍。英文意思為 *enter a place or a specific area*。

Derek opens the door and <u>gets in</u> the back seat.
（德瑞克打開車門並進到後座。）

- **get in** 抵達、到達某個地方。英文意思為 *arrive at a place or a specific area*。

My relatives <u>get in town</u> at midnight for an examination test the next day.

（為了隔天的入學考試，我的親戚們半夜時抵達市區。）

- **get in** 取得錄取資格。英文意思為 *become accepted.*。

Unfortunately, Derek didn't <u>get in the law school</u> he applied.

（不幸的是，德瑞克並沒有錄取他申請的法學院。）

unit 08

Eva Moves In Mark's Apartment.
同居了

片語搶先看

1. move in 搬進新居	2. be devoted to 獻身於、致力於
3. mean the world to somebody 對某人來説很重要、你是我的一切	4. feel like doing something 想要、意欲做某事
5. make noises 發出噪音	6. laugh at 嘲笑

看對話學英文

In the third month of their relationship, Eva moves in Mark's apartment.

在交往的第三個月，伊娃搬進了馬可的公寓。

E ▶ Eva 伊娃　　　**M** ▶ Mark 馬可

E I was already so surprised when you made a copy of your keys for me. And now we live together.

（在你給我一份你家的鑰匙的時候我就很震驚了，現在我們竟然住在一起了。）

M It was in my plan. I want to share everything with you.

（那在我的計劃之中，我想要跟你分享我的所有。）

Eva quickly kisses Mark on the cheek, and she imitates the way he talks to her.

伊娃飛快地親吻馬可的臉頰，並且模仿他對她說話的樣子。

E I said I would be devoted to you.

（我說我會全心全意對你的。）

M You always knew what I am going to say.

（你總是知道我想說什麼。）

E But I want to know the reason behind the answer. Tell me, why do you treat me so nicely?

（但是我想要知道背後的原因，告訴我，為什麼要對我那麼好？）

M Because I love you. You mean the world to me.

（因為我愛你，你就是我的全世界。）

E I love you, too.

（我也愛你。）

Mark Cooper, an exceptional entrepreneur for his employees and an enigmatic tycoon for the public, is now making a chicken sandwich for Eva. She feels it so surrealistic.

馬可庫柏，一位對員工來說是位傑出的企業家，對社會大眾來說是個神秘的企業大亨，現在正在為伊娃做雞肉沙拉，她覺得好不真實。

Ⓔ You are so different when you are at home. I like that.

（你在家裡跟你在外面表現差好多，我喜歡這樣。）

Ⓜ Only for you.

（你專屬的喔。）

Mark is tasting the flavor of the chicken.

馬可正在嚐雞肉的味道。

Ⓔ I like the way you make noises when you chew.

（你咬東西發出的怪聲好可愛喔。）

Ⓜ Don't laugh at me. Come here and have a bite.

（別嘲笑我了，過來吃一口看看。）

Ⓔ I think one more teaspoon of mayonnaise will make the salad perfect.

（我覺得再加一小匙美乃滋，沙拉就完美了。）

片語有道理

常跟你相處的朋友或親人，會跟你有相同的生活經驗，這些相同的經驗，可以作為生活中的溝通基礎，更可以用來互開玩笑。在英文中，開玩笑說法有 laugh at 嘲笑、tease 戲弄、make fun of 取笑和 mock 嘲弄：

laugh at 嘲笑，對某件嚴重或應該嚴肅看待的事情一笑置之。英文意思為 *make a joke of something that is serious or should be taken seriously*，例如當你的朋友很嚴肅的跟你說他的病情時，你卻用詼諧的方式看待，惹得你的朋友也變得不那麼嚴肅了。

It's not easy to be comedians because they have to <u>make people laugh at their pain.</u>

（當喜劇人員並不容易，因為他們必須要讓大家笑看人生悲劇。）

tease 取笑戲弄，拿別人的事情開玩笑。英文意思為 *to laugh at or make jokes about somebody in a friendly way in order to embarrass them*，可以指朋友間友善的玩笑或逗弄，在友善的前提下可以視為一種情感增進的方法。

Nowadays, the young like to <u>tease each other</u> to enhance friendship.

（現在的年輕人喜歡透過開玩笑的方式增進友誼。）

---

make fun of 取笑。英文意思為 to laugh at or make jokes about somebody in an unfriendly way，以令人不舒服的方式取笑他人。

Anita's American boyfriend likes to make fun of her family's Taiwanese accent when they speak English.

（艾妮塔的美國男友喜歡取笑她家人說英文時的台灣腔。）

---

mock 模仿他人以達到取笑的目的。英文意思為 to laugh at somebody or something by copying what they say or do in an unfriendly way，模仿他人以達到取笑的目的，通常是以讓人不舒服的方式。

The stay-at-home mom becomes popular after she mocked a politician on a talk show.

（那位家庭主婦自從在一個節目模仿政治家後，就紅了起來。）

一字多義

♠ **move in** 搬家、**step in** 出手幫忙、**jump in** 插話

move（移動）、step（踏步）、jump（跳躍）都是指身體的動作，
但搭配介係詞 in（進入……），意思就不只是身體的動作那麼單純了：

- **move** 變換身體的姿勢、移動。**move in** 搬進新居，英
  文意思為 To begin living in a new place。

  A celebrity <u>moves in</u> the community last month.

  （一位名流上個月搬進了這個社區。）

- **step** 將腳抬起、踏步。**step in** 介入、出手幫忙，英文意
  思為 to become involved in a difficult situation in
  order to offer help。

  When do the social workers think it's time to <u>step in</u> for stray
  dogs?

  （社工人員什麼時候覺得是時候該出手解決流浪狗的問題呢？）

- **jump** 利用腿跟腳快速離開地面、跳躍。**jump in** 插話，
  通常是插入跟原本對話無關的主題，英文意思為 To
  interrupt others' conversation.

  Sorry I have to <u>jump in</u> here.

  （抱歉，我必須在這邊打斷一下。）

A Relationship Goes In Circles.
鬼打牆的交往關係

 片語搶先看

1. bring up 談到	2. every now and then 偶爾
3. keep in mind 記住	4. go in circles 說話／做事一直重複卻沒達到效果（鬼打牆）
5. take a rain check 延遲	

 看對話學英文

There was one thing that bothers Eva a lot- Mark and she are living separate lives. She often found her alone doing laundry or scrubbing the floor at home while Mark went out to the gym. Eva brings up this issue every now and then, but it seems that Mark just doesn't keep it in mind. This is how the relationship of the couples goes in cirlces. On Friday night, the couples cuddle on the couch in the living room,

有一件事情讓伊娃非常煩心，那就是他們各過各的生活。她發現自己常

Ep 2 : Getting Close Or Distant ／越來越好，還是漸行漸遠？
Unit 9 A Relationship Goes In Circles. ／鬼打牆的交往關係

PART 1 圖解介系詞篇

PART 2 看故事學片語篇

常週末在家洗衣服或刷地板，而馬可則待在健身中心，伊娃偶爾會提到這個議題，但是馬可似乎沒有放在心上，這對情侶的關係開始變得有點鬼打牆。週五晚上，這對情侶在客廳的沙發上依偎著。

E ▶ Eva 伊娃　　　**M** ▶ Mark 馬可

E What's our plan tomorrow? Can we do what couples do, like going to a late night movie?

（我們明天的計畫是什麼？我們能像一般情侶約會那樣嗎？晚場電影好嗎？）

M I have to go to the gym tomorrow. Can we take a rain check?

（我明天要去運動中心，我們改天好嗎？）

E Fine. I would just watch TV at home.

（好吧，我就在家看電視好了。）

On Saturday morning, the couples are having corn soup at the dinning table in the kitchen.

週六早晨，這對情侶在廚房的餐桌上喝玉米湯。

E Let's go jogging after the breakfast.

（吃完早餐我們去晨跑吧。）

M I would love to go, but honey, I am going to the gym.

（我很想去，但我要去健身中心。）

E Jogging burns calorie as well.

（慢跑也可以消耗熱量。）

Ⓜ That's different from the muscle-building workout.

（但是跟鍛鍊肌肉是不一樣的。）

Ⓔ I think we do not spend enough time together. You are always so busy at work, and you stay at the gym when you are free.

（我覺得我們得找時間多相處，你上班總是很忙，而一下班就又總在健身中心。）

Ⓜ I just need to go to the gym where I can fully relax.

（我需要去健身中心，因為在那邊我可以完全的放鬆。）

Ⓔ I feel we are so far apart, even though we are physically close. I want your company. Don't you understand?

（即使我們靠的那麼近，但我覺得我們好遙遠，我想要你的陪伴，你不懂嗎？）

Ⓜ Can't I have some time alone?

（我難道不能有一些獨處的時間嗎？）

Mark remains insistent on this issue, which makes Eva feel heartbroken.

馬可持續堅持己見，讓伊娃傷透了心。

表達延緩、延期的片語：*take a rain check* 延遲做某事

I can't come to the interview Friday but I hope you'll give me a rain check.

（星期五的面試我無法赴約，我希望你可以讓我延期。）

註 此片語的來源是過去舉行棒球賽，遇到突然下雨得取消比賽的情況時，主辦單位就會提供 rain check 給球迷，讓他們下次可以憑票觀賞補賽，後來 rain check 引申為當事人可以在未來的某個時間點再來進行本來要進行的活動：

語氣與文法：

碰上別人的邀約時，你因為時間無法配合而要求延期，在社交上可能會某種程度上造成別人的麻煩，因此常常會搭配表示禮貌的用語：sorry（抱歉），在文法上，會用 *will / be going to*（未來式）表示自己未來無法配合，也常會使用 *have to*（情態助動詞）來表達一定要延期之不得已的狀況：

Sorry, I am too tired today. I will have to take a rain check.

（抱歉，我今天太累了，可以改期嗎？）

換句話說來表達延遲之意：postpone 延緩做某事、推遲，英文意思為 to arrange an event to take place at a later time，字根 post 即為 after，在……後的意思。

The release of new smart phone is postponed due to financial issues.

（新手機的推出因為財務問題而延遲了。）

註 be put off 用法類似於 be postponed，表達被延遲的意思。

一字多義

♠ bring 帶來、bring up 提出、bring out 凸顯

- **bring** 常見的意思為帶來、拿來，英文意思為 come to a place with someone or something，常見的口語用法有：

❶ Bring an umbrella with you.

（記得帶傘。）

❷ I'll bring my boyfriend tonight.

（晚上我會攜伴喔。）

- **bring** 應用到片語 **bring up** 提出某議題、**bring out** 凸顯某特徵時，表達 **present**（呈現出）的意思：

  ❶ bring up something / bring something up

  （提出某議題）

  ❷ It's inappropriate to bring up a sensitive subject at a business meeting.

  （在商務會議中提出敏感的議題並不恰當。）

  ❸ I can't believe that Lisa just brought it up at the meeting!

  （麗莎竟然在會議中提出這個！）

- **bring out something (in somebody)** 帶出某人……的一面。

  ❶ Pressure can bring out the worst or the best in people.

  （壓力可以看出一個人最差或最好的一面。）

  ❷ Competition can bring out your strength.

  （競爭可以帶出你的實力。）

We Need To Talk.
我們來談談吧！

片語搶先看

1. be made for each other 天造地設的一對	2. break up 分手
3. up to someone 由某人決定	4. no matter 不論
5. be fed up with something 因某事而厭煩、受夠了	6. turn around 轉身

看對話學英文

Sweet and torturous memories flash through Eva's mind; all those memories were full of the laughter, tears, and kissing. Tears soon came out from her eyes. Eva decides to tell Mark how she feels.

甜蜜又折磨人心的記憶反覆出現在伊娃心中，那些充滿笑容、淚水與親吻的回憶。眼淚在她的眼眶打轉，伊娃決定告訴馬可她的感受。

E ▶ Eva 伊娃　　　**M** ▶ Mark 馬可

E Do you have a moment? We need to talk.

（你有時間嗎？我想要談談。）

M Yes, of course. What's wrong? You look uneasy.

（當然，你還好嗎？你看起來很不安。）

E I don't feel satisfied.

（我覺得不滿足。）

M What do you mean?

（什麼意思？）

E I don't think we are made for each other. I don't think this is going anywhere. We are just too different.

（我覺得我們不適合，這段感情不會有結果的，我們太不相同了。）

M If breaking up can make you happy, then we will do it.

（如果你覺得分手會讓你快樂，那我們就這麼做。）

E Don't you have any words for me? Aren't you asking me why?

（你沒有什麼要對我說的嗎？難道你不問我為什麼嗎？）

M I would respect your decision.

（我尊重你的決定。）

E We are supposed to be each other's partners sharing life and everything. But you are already so busy for your huge business. And you even choose to spend your work-free time at the gym for hours...

PART 1 圖解介系詞篇

PART 2 看故事學片語篇

（我們應該是彼此的伴侶，分享所有的生活，你已經為了你龐大的事業非常忙碌了，但你甚至連沒有上班的時間都窩在健身中心好幾個小時⋯⋯。）

Ⓜ If you want to find others to be your partner, just go.

（如果你想找其他人做你的伴侶，去吧。）

Ⓔ Don't you ask me to stay?

（你不挽留我嗎？）

Ⓜ It's up to you. No matter what I say, you've made your decision already.

（這是你的決定，不管我說什麼，你已經決定了。）

Ⓔ I knew you are fed up.

（我就知道你受夠這段感情了。）

Eva turns around and leaves.

伊娃轉身離去。

 片語有道理

當遇到你不開心的事情時，你會覺得厭煩，覺得受夠了！在英文中，表達這種不耐煩的情緒有：

> *fed up* 形容詞，需搭配 *be* 動詞使用，英文意思為 *be bored with something that you can't bear any longer*，表達某事長期讓你感到厭煩、受夠了。

The student is fed up with the cramming style of teaching.

（學生受夠了填鴨式的教學。）

> *tire of* 動詞片語，不需搭配 *be* 動詞，意指感到厭煩，英文意思為 *be bored with something/someone*，表達對某事失去興趣、耐性，並覺得無聊了。

Alice would soon tired of her new boyfriend.

（愛麗絲很快就會對她的新男友感到厭倦了。）

> *sick of* 形容詞，需搭配 *be* 動詞使用，英文意思為 *be annoyed with something that happens continuously which you want it to stop*，對某個持續很久又沒有改善的情況，而感到厭煩。

I am sick of your moaning and groaning. Stop it!

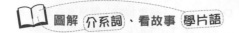

（你的嗚噎抱怨令我厭煩。快停止！）

其他表示厭煩的用語與例句：

❶ You annoyed me.

（你很煩。）

❷ I am sick to death of all of you.

（你整個人都令人覺得噁心。）

❸ I've had enough of your garbage.

（我受夠了。）

 一字多義

♠ break up 分手、break down 壞掉

- **break up** 分手，一段感情的結束，例如：婚姻、戀愛等。

  ❶ For Josh, she is his only girlfriend. He will never break up with her and love her to death.

  （對喬許來說，她是他唯一的女友，他對她的愛至死不渝，絕對不會跟她分手。）

❷ Camille feels guilty for having an affair with his boss and <u>breaking up</u> his family.

（卡蜜兒對於自己跟老闆發生婚外情，並破壞別人的家庭感到愧疚。）

- **break down** 壞掉，指機器或車輛因為某個零件或系統無法運作而壞掉了。也表達人的理智斷線，情緒失去控制的狀況。

❶ The electric power system <u>has broken down</u> because of the typhoon.

（電力系統因為颱風而故障了。）

❷ When the woman's son died from liver cancer, she started to <u>break down</u> and cry.

（當那女人的兒子死於肝癌時，她失控地大哭。）

Eva Bursts Out Crying.
大哭特哭！

 片語搶先看

1. head back 打道回府	2. burst out crying 突然大哭
3. cannot help but do something 不得不	4. move on 繼續前進
5. come and pass 發生	

看對話學英文

Eva heads back to the apartment after the quarrel. Eve lets her tears cross all over her face. Renee is surprised to see her crying.

伊娃在爭吵後返回公寓，伊娃任由淚水流滿面，芮妮很驚訝看到伊娃哭著回家。

E ▶ Eva 伊娃　　　**R** ▶ Renee 芮妮

R Is everything all right? Your eyes are filled with tears.

（你還好嗎？怎麼哭了？）

E I broke up with Mark.

（我跟馬可分手了。）

R It must be painful.

（你一定很難過。）

Eva drags her feet to the bathroom. She looks at her pathetic face in the mirror.

伊娃拖著腳步走到浴室，看著鏡子裡自己可憐兮兮的臉。

E Will I ever be happy again?

（我還能夠幸福嗎？）

R You knew you will. Come here.

（你知道你會的。過來。）

Renee hugs Eva, and Eva bursts out crying.

芮妮抱住伊娃，伊娃突然大哭了起來。

E I knew this relationship is not going to work no matter how hard I try. But I just can't help but cry when it ends.

（我知道即使我再努力，這段感情也不會有結果的。但我還是忍不住在感情結束時哭泣。）

Ⓡ Just move on.

（往前看吧。）

Ⓔ I feel the void in my chest.

（我覺得好空虛。）

Ⓡ It's one of the phases after a breakup, and you should just let it come and pass.

（這是分手後的階段之一，它會來、也會走的。）

Ⓔ It's easier said than done.

（説的比做的容易。）

Ⓡ You should try to face your grief and deal with it.

（至少你得試著面對自己的悲傷，並且治好它。）

Ⓔ I'll be fine, won't I?

（我會沒事的，對吧？）

Ⓡ Of course. You won't die from a broken heart.

（當然，傷心不會死人的。）

Ep 2：Getting Close Or Distant ╱越來越好，還是漸行漸遠？
Unit 11 Eva Bursts Out Crying. ╱大哭特哭！

1 PART
圖解介系詞篇

2 PART
看故事學片語篇

 片語有道理

表達情緒激動，無法控制、避免某些情況的發生時：

---

cannot help but do something 不得不做某事，英文意思為 *it is impossible to prevent something to happen*。例如你因為某個笑話而大笑出聲，或因為某事特別，而忍不住偷看；因為某個疑點而忍不住懷疑、因為開心忍不住感到驕傲時，都是用這個句型：

---

❶ Richard <u>cannot help but glance at the person</u> who wears sweater in a hot summer day.

（理查忍不住看了那個在大熱天穿著毛衣的人一眼。）

❷ Sean <u>cannot help but feel proud of himself</u> winning "The Putting-the-Most-Layers-of-Clothing Competition" in a hot summer day.

（尚恩忍不住為自己贏得「在大熱天穿最多衣服之競賽」，感到驕傲。）

---

burst out doing something 突然做某事而無法自己停止，例如突然大笑或大哭，英文意思為 *to make sounds all of a sudden and could not stop oneself.*

---

❶ Sean's family <u>burst out laughing</u> when they heard of the

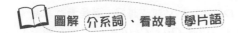

story of the trophy and the competition.

（尚恩的家人聽到比賽與獎盃的故事後，忍不住大笑出聲。）

❷ Sean was offended and <u>burst out crying</u>.

（尚恩覺得被冒犯了，開始突然大哭。）

♠ move on 繼續前進、move in 搬進新居、move out 搬出來

- **move on** 繼續前進、著手做下一件事，英文意思為 *to start doing something new*，可以指一段感情結束後開始過新的生活，也可以指會議中進行到下一個議題等。

  ❶ The widower's wife had been dead for a year now. It was time for him to forget the past and <u>move on</u>.

  （這個鰥夫的太太已經過世一年了，是時候他應該忘記過去開始新生活了。）

  ❷ We shouldn't waste time on the insignificant problems, so let's <u>move on</u> to some other issues.

  （我們不要在雞毛蒜皮的議題上浪費時間了，我們討論其他的議題吧。）

1 PART 圖解介系詞篇

2 PART 看故事學片語篇

- **move in** 搬進新居，對搬家的人而言，不管搬到朋友的公寓（friend's flat）或是剛落成的新家（a new home），都是一個新環境、新居。

  Our new neighbor <u>moves in</u> around the 22nd of the month.

  （我們的新鄰居大概這個月的 22 號搬進來。）

- **move in with somebody** 搬到某人的家，而那個人原本就住在那裡，例如：你的阿姨家是獨棟透天，有很多間空房，她說你可以去住，這時你就可以說：

  I am <u>moving in with</u> my aunt.

  （我要搬去跟我的阿姨住。）

- **move out** 搬出去，搬離一個舊的居所。

  My wife and I decide to <u>move out of</u> my parent's house.

  （我跟我太太決定要搬離父母的家裡。）

Move On
重新開始

片語搶先看

1. have no choice but to do something 不得不做某事	2. wear somebody out 使某人筋疲力竭
3. be all set to do something 準備做某事	4. to be cut out for 適合做某事
5. have one's heart set on 渴望、傾心於	6. set forth 啟程、動身

看對話學英文

Eva and Renee are hanging out in the living room.

伊娃與芮妮在客廳裡消磨時間。

E ▶ Eva 伊娃　　　**R** ▶ Renee 芮妮

E I miss him so much. I have no choice but to keep thinking of him, and that really wears me out. The thought of having a future without him is frightening.

（我真的很想他，我沒有辦法控制自己不想他，但這也讓我筋疲力竭。想到沒有他的未來我就很害怕。）

R Eva, you should look ahead instead of looking back.

（你真的應該要往前看，而不是活在過去。）

E I know that I should move on. But I can't.

（我知道我應該開始新生活，但是我做不到。）

R If you decide to live in the past, I would let you.

（如果你想要活在過去，我也不會阻止你。）

E Alright.

（好嘛。）

R This is life. Think of other beautiful things in the world.

（這就是人生，想想世界上其他美麗的事物吧。）

E I need to cheer up!

（我必須打起精神來。）

R That's right! Just be all set to start your new life without him. And you will believe in love, couplehood, and partnership again.

（這就對了，從新開始沒有他的生活吧，你會再度對愛情、情侶、人生夥伴感到信心的。）

E Look at you. You are cut out for being a love consoler.

（你看你，根本天生就是愛情諮詢師。）

🅡 So now have your heart set on a whole new life. I am going to do community service this weekend. Come with me.

（所以妳現在必須讓自己對於新生活感到渴望。這禮拜我要去做社區服務，跟我一起去吧。）

🅔 I would rather stay at home.

（我比較想要待在家。）

🅡 For what? Crying for your loss? The relationship of you and Mark is now history. Come on!

（待在家幹嘛？為你所失去的哭泣嗎？少來了，你跟馬可的感情已經是歷史了。）

🅔 Alright. I will go with you.

（好吧，我會跟你去。）

🅡 Great. We will set forth at 9 a.m. I will drive.

（很好，那我們早上九點出發，我開車。）

 片語有道理

專業來自於對某個領域的專精，需要很多時間的投入，若沒有興趣，則很難出神入化，也就是說興趣與專業是息息相關的，表達專業與興趣的英文片語有：

> 表達對某事物有興趣、充滿熱情的片語 1：**show an interest in something** 對……有興趣

Elliot grew up at a time when most boys usually <u>showed an interest in</u> science.

（艾略特處於的世代，是大部分的男孩都對科學有興趣。）

> 表達對某事物有興趣、充滿熱情的片語 2：**have a passion for something** 對……充滿熱情

Abby <u>has a passion for</u> dance. For her, dance is her soul and she cannot live without it.

（艾比對舞蹈充滿熱情。對她來說舞蹈是她的靈魂，是生命中不可分割的一部分。）

> 表達致力於做某事、對某事投入很多心力之片語 1：**devote oneself to** 獻身於

Pan decided to leave his full-time job and <u>devote himself to</u>

making coffee a billion-dollar business.

（潘決定要辭去他的工作，以投入他的億萬咖啡事業。）

表達致力於做某事、對某事投入很多心力之片語 2：**have one's heart set on** 渴望、傾心於

The contestant insists that she doesn't <u>have her heart set on</u> winning the World Martial Arts Tournament.

（那位參賽者堅持，她參加世界第一武道會的目的並不是得冠軍。）

表達適合某事物，可以指職業、某方面有才能、或是某種生活環境的片語 1：**be cut out for something** 適合……某事物

I hate big cities and public transportation. I think <u>I am just cut out for</u> small-town living.

（我討厭大城市跟大眾運輸系統，我想我比較適合小鎮生活。）

表達適合某事物，可以指職業、某方面有才能、或是某種生活環境的片語 2：*be cut out to be* 在……方面有才能

Robert <u>is not really cut out to</u> be a novelist. People say his works are more like a collection of essays than novels.

（羅伯特沒有小說家的才能，人們說他的作品比較像是散文的選集而不是小說。）

一字多義

♠ wear out 使……筋疲力竭、wear off 漸漸消逝

- **wear out** 使……疲累，如持續長時間做某事而感到累。英文意思為 *feel tired or exhausted by doing too much of something.*

  ❶ I could never be a nanny because <u>kids could really wear me out</u>.

  （我永遠都不可能當保母的，因為小孩們弄得我筋疲力竭。）

  ❷ My goal is to <u>wear out my running shoes</u> on the treadmill.

  （我的目標是要在跑步機上把我慢跑鞋穿壞。）

- **wear off** 漸漸消失，如某種情緒的消退、或是藥效的消退。英文意思為 *to gradually stop existing.*

  ❶ Having a new roommate could be exciting, but <u>the novelty could soon wear off</u>.

  （有新室友是讓人興奮的，但是新鮮感可能很快就消失了。）

  ❷ Once <u>the effects of pills wear off</u>, you might start feeling hurt again.

  （當藥效退去後，你可能會繼續感到痛。）

Part 1 圖解介系詞篇

Part 2 看故事學片語篇

unit 13

Bump Into The Ex-Boyfriend
巧遇前男友

 片語搶先看

1. How's everything? 最近好嗎？	2. sign up 報名、簽約
3. fill out 填寫	4. bump into 巧遇
5. drop in on someone 偶訪（人）	6. Are you nuts? 你瘋了嗎？

 看對話學英文

Renee parks her car at Light House, an orphanage in Muzha, Taipei. At the front door, an amiable lady is welcoming the visitors.

芮妮把她的車子停在光明之家，台北木柵的一家孤兒院，院門口站著一位和藹的女人歡迎著訪客。

E ▶ Eva 伊娃　　**R** ▶ Renee 芮妮

C ▶ Caroline 卡洛琳　　**M** ▶ Mark 馬可

C Welcome ladies. I am the principle of Light House.

（歡迎小姐們，我是光明之家的院長。）

R Hi, Caroline. How's everything?

（嗨卡洛琳，最近好嗎？）

C We're fine.

（我們很好。）

E I'm Eva. Nice to meet you.

（我是伊娃，很高興認識你。）

C Thank you for signing up for the volunteer program. Please fill out the form for the basic information first.

（謝謝你報名志工服務，請你先填寫基本資料。）

E Sure.

（好的。）

Eva and Renee follows Caroline to a meeting room.

伊娃與芮妮跟著卡洛琳往會議室走去。

C We are hosting a charity fair on Thanksgiving. We would love to have you and other volunteers assist in planning this fair.

（我們要在感恩節舉辦議一場慈善義賣會，很開心有你們參與幫忙規劃這場義賣會。）

E Sounds exciting.

（聽起來很棒。）

C Please take a seat. We'll start the meeting soon.

（請先坐一下，會議很快就要開始了。）

Before the meeting, Eva goes to the lady's room. She bumps into a man and finds a familiar face.

在會議開始之前，伊娃去了一趟洗手間，在路上她巧遇一個臉龐令她熟悉的男子。

E Mark?

（馬可？）

M Eva? What are you doing here?

（伊娃？你怎麼會在這？）

E I am a volunteer here. And you?

（我在這裡當志工，你呢？）

M I drop in on Caroline often. Let me drive you home after that.

（我常來這裡拜訪卡洛琳。結束後我載妳回去吧。）

E Sure.（Why do I say yes? Are you nuts?）

（好啊。（我怎麼會答應他？你瘋了嗎？））

Mark winks at her and leaves.

馬可朝她眨眨眼就離開了。

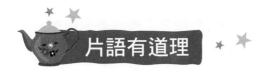

片語有道理

人與人之間的對話大多以打招呼開始的，打招呼的用語會因為對象、熟悉度，以及場合而有些差異：

> 休閒、非正式的場合：

❶ 遇到熟人時的打招呼用語："Hey"。

❷ 跟戀人、朋友在見面時、使用簡訊或網路聊天時："Hey there"。

❸ 在跟同輩的朋友、同事、或兄弟姊妹在休閒的場合打招呼，也可以用在路上碰面匆匆打招呼，雖然是問句，但不需要實際回答："Hey! What's up?"、"How are things?"、"How are you?"。

> 在休閒、非正式的場合跟很久沒見的朋友寒暄：

❶ 放鬆非正式的場合，遇到你很久沒有看到的朋友、同事、或家人時："Good to see you"、"Great to see you,"、"Nice to see you."。

❷ 遇到好久不見的朋友，充滿興奮感的打招呼方式："Look who it is!"。

> 正式的場合：

❶ 非常正式的問候語，如在電影中機器人對主人的用語，若想要在對話中用復古的方式增添樂趣時可以使用："Greeting."。

❷ 在餐廳中、飯店、購物中心服務員對顧客間或是工作場合與同事的招呼用語，屬於較為正式的用語："Good morning"、"Good afternoon"、"Good evening."。

❸ 在專業人士的聚會場所，或是廠商與顧客間、上司與下屬在工作場合的正式問候："How are you doing today?"

一字多義

♠ 拜訪 drop in、退出 drop out

· **drop in on somebody** 拜訪，*drop* 表達為了去目的地而停車之意；**drop in on** 表示拜訪某人，特別是沒有事先講好短暫的拜訪，也可以指隨意參與課程：

❶ Please make sure the social workers <u>drop in on Mr. Fortner</u> every now and then.

（請確保社工人員會偶爾造訪福特納先生。）

❷ The exchange students from Europe attend lectures and <u>drop in on classes</u>.

（歐洲來的交換學生參加講座和旁聽課程。）

- **drop out of something** 退出，*drop* 表達停止做某件事，**drop out** 表示退出某個課程、不再參與某個計畫、退學，英文意思為 *to stop taking part in something.*。

❶ The student <u>dropped out of school</u> because his academic performance was affected by bullying.

（那位學生因為學業成績受霸凌影響，退學了。）

❷ People are curious about the reasons why Mandy <u>drops out of college</u> two years later.

（大家很好奇曼蒂在兩年後休學的原因。）

Going Back Together Again?
要復合嗎？

 片語搶先看

1. get nervous 緊張	2. gaze at 凝視
3. stir up 引起、惹起、鼓勵	4. take a walk 散步
5. take somebody back 接受某人（特別指離開某段關係、戀情後再次接受）	6. cast a spell 施咒、讓某人無法招架

看對話學英文

Eva comes back to the meeting room.

伊娃走回會議室。

E ▶ Eva 伊娃　**R** ▶ Renee 芮妮　**M** ▶ Mark 馬可

R Hurry up!

（快點！）

E I am coming. You wouldn't believe who I ran into. It was Mark.

（我這就來了。你一定不敢相信我遇到誰，是馬可。）

R Your ex? What the hell!

（你的前男友？也太衰了。）

Mark walks into the room. Eva whispers to Renee.

馬可也走進會議室，伊娃對芮妮講悄悄話。

E Oh my god! It is him.

（天啊！真的是他。）

R Gosh. Is the destiny playing a joke on you ?

（天啊！你跟他真的是冤家。）

After the meeting, Eva finds that Mark is waiting for her at the front gate. She is getting nervous; her heart beats fast, and her palm sweats. She greets with her voice cracking.

會議結束後，伊娃看到馬可在前門等她。她開始緊張了，她心跳加快，手掌出汗，她試著打招呼，聲音卻有點沙啞。

E How have you been?

（你好嗎？）

Ⓜ Not very well.

（不是很好。）

Marks gazes at Eva, which stirs up her bitter-sweet memories.

馬可凝視著伊娃，激起伊娃過去又苦又甜的回憶。

Ⓜ Shall we take a walk?

（我們去散步好嗎？）

Eva feels the electricity is flowing between them, and she nods.

伊娃感受到兩個人間的電流，她點頭答應。

Ⓜ Can you take me back?

（你願意再次接受我嗎？）

Mark still affects Eva.

馬可仍然影響著伊娃。

Ⓔ When can you stop casting a spell on me?

（你還要對我施展魔咒到什麼時候？）

A huge grin appears on Mark's face.

馬可臉上露出開心的笑容。

片語有道理

get 做連綴動詞用時表達「狀態之意」，英文意思為 to start to be in a particular condition，表達某人或某事開始進入另一種特定的狀態、情緒等，相關的用法有：

---

get nervous 變得緊張

The girl <u>gets nervous</u> when talking to strangers.

（這個女孩跟陌生人說話時會緊張。）

> 註 「get＋形容詞」表達從原本的某狀態，進入到另一種狀態，有「切換到⋯⋯情緒」的意味，以本例句來說，女孩從原本不緊張，到一碰到陌生人就變得緊張的狀態。

---

get pageant 懷孕了

It's common that many couples <u>get pregnant</u> before marriage.

（情侶未婚懷孕這件事很常見。）

---

get fat 變胖

If you don't reduce alcohol and caffeine in your diet, you can easily get <u>fat</u>.

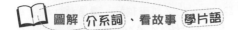

（如果你不將酒精與咖啡因從你的飲食中去除，你會很容易變胖。）

get angry 生氣了

The girl who is boiled gets angry when being ignored.

（那個有公主病的女孩被人忽略的時候會生氣。）

get better 好轉

Sara ran a fever last night, but she is getting better now.

（莎拉昨晚發高燒，但是她現在好多了。）

get bored 感到無聊

Hank gets bored when studying by himself, so he joins a study group.

（漢克覺得自己讀書很無聊，所以他加入讀書會。）

 一字多義

♠ stir in 拌入、stir up 惹起

- **stir in** 拌入，指實際上的動作，英文意思為 *to mix something thoroughly*，將食物攪拌均勻，*stir in* 常出現在烹調用語。

❶ Gabi <u>stirs in</u> mashed potato and mushroom and cooks until they become golden. It takes around 8 minutes.

（佳比拌入馬鈴薯泥跟蘑菇泥並且煮到金黃色，大約需要八分鐘。）

❷ The next step on the recipe is to <u>stir in</u> 1 table spoon of butter.

（食譜的下一步要你加入一湯匙的奶油。）

- **stir up** 引起、惹起、鼓勵，指情緒的波動，英文意思為 *to affect something strongly*，引起某人在某方面的強烈感受，**也可以專指引發麻煩、爭吵、問題等負面的事件**，英文意思為 *to cause trouble, arguments, or problems*。

❶ The candidate of 2012 presidential election <u>stirred up</u> a national discussion on parenting.

（2012 年的總統大選候選人引起全國對父母與孩子教養的討論。）

❷ The woman was reluctant to say yes because she didn't want to <u>stir up</u> more trouble for herself.

（那個女人不願意答應，因為她不想再給自己找更多麻煩了。）

Starting A New Job
開始新工作

片語搶先看

1. call on 短暫的拜訪某人	2. get up 起床
3. put on 穿戴衣服、帽子等	4. turn on 播放
5. get on 上車	6. get out of/ get off 下車
7. take off 脫掉衣服或帽子	8. turn off 關閉電源

看日記學英文

Starting a new job is already stressful itself. Not to mention that I start a job as a sale representative in a bustling city, which makes me even more nervous. I am new at work, not equipping with powerful selling skills yet. But I still have to gain those skills no matter what. What I have to do every day is to visit a lot of strangers. My boss calls them potential customers. My plan today is to call on Mr. Steinfeld at seven a.m. in the

Ep 3：A Job, A Career, Or A Calling? ╱ 一份工作、一份職業，還是一個志業？
Unit 01 Starting A New Job ╱ 開始新工作

1 PART
圖解介系詞篇

2 PART
看故事學片語篇

morning. Who will go to work so early? Whatever. Because of the appointment, I got up very early and put on the most decent suit. Mr. Steinfeld's factory is located at the far east area, producing every kind of knitting hats. My goal is to persuade him to buy the service from FFI, a package delivery company that I work for. Before I really met the guy and achieved the goal, I travelled 40 miles by bus first to reach the factory. To entertain myself, I turned on the radio and then got on the bus. After an hour and half, the bus stopped, I got off the bus, and for a better business look, I took off my scarf and hat. The radio was also turned off for a positive work attitude.

　　開始新工作這件事本身就是讓人感到有壓力的事情，更別說我的新工作是在一個忙碌城市中的一名業務，這讓我的壓力更大。我是職場新鮮人，還沒有超強銷售技巧。但是不管怎樣我還是要有那些能力，每天我的工作就是要見很多陌生人，而我的老闆稱他們為潛力客戶。我今天的任務是要在早上七點拜訪史坦菲德先生。誰那麼早去工作啊？算了，隨便。由於跟客戶有約，我很早就起床並且穿上我最體面的西裝。史坦菲德先生的工廠在很遠的西邊，製造各式各樣的針織帽。而我今天的目標是要說服他買我們 FFI 服務，FFI 就是我所服務的一間快遞公司。在我能見到他並達成目標之前，我得先搭公車走 40 哩的路才能到達工廠，為了讓搭公車也具娛樂性，我先打開廣播，才上公車。過一個半小時之後，公車停了，我下了公車，為了讓自己看起來更專業，我把圍巾跟帽子拿下，當然我也把音樂關了，以展現積極的態度。

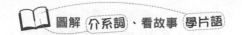

 片語有道理

搭乘交通公工具的常見動詞用法有 board 搭乘 、get in/ into 搭乘、get on/onto 搭乘，三種用法上有些微的差異，請見下列例子：

> **board** 可作為及物與不及物動詞，表搭乘某交通工具之意：

❶ Passengers will have to have a ticket in order to <u>board the train</u>.

（乘客必須要有車票才可以搭乘火車。）

❷ After the burglar stole paintings from the museum, he tried to <u>board the bus</u> to escape.

（在竊賊從博物館偷走名畫之後，他試著上公車逃逸。）

❸ My boss is supposed to <u>board</u> at 9:30.

（我的老闆應該在九點半就上車了。）

> 「**get on**＋交通工具」表搭乘某交通工之意，介系詞 **on** 之後必須加交通工具。當你搭乘的交通工具的空間較為開放時使用，例如：你可以在火車上走動、坐下、甚至有些火車是有臥鋪可以讓你躺下的。

❶ Mars <u>get on a train</u> nervously.

（馬爾斯緊張地上火車。）

❷ Before we <u>get on the plane</u>, we have to wait in line for boarding.

（在我們上飛機之前，我們必須先排隊登機。）

> 「*get in*＋交通工具」表搭乘某交通工之意，介系詞 *in* 之後必須加交通工具。當你搭乘的交通工具空間較小、沒辦法讓你隨意走動或站立時使用。

❶ I saw Molly <u>got in a red car</u> yesterday.

（我看見茉莉昨天上了一台紅色的車。）

❷ This is the first time I <u>get in a real helicopter</u>.

（這是我第一次搭真的直升機。）

♠ get up 起床、wake up 醒來

- **get up** 起床，英文意思為 *get out of bed*，也就是從床上起來之意，你可能會常聽到別人問你：

When did you <u>get up</u> today?

（你今天幾點起床？）

I <u>got up</u> at six.

（我六點起床。）

➤ 你也可以這麼回答：

I <u>wake up</u> at six this morning.

（我今天早上六點醒來。）

解析

get 表示身體離開床的物理現象，所以當你 **get up** 時，你的腦袋不一定清醒，而當你 **wake up** 時，你可以躺在床上，或是離開床了，可以確定的是你的心靈上已經清醒，也準備迎接一天的挑戰了。

- **wake up** 醒來，英文意思為 *become more lively*，除了表達從睡夢中甦醒，也可以用來表示清醒之意，例如沖個冷水澡可以讓頭腦清醒。

Before Jamie goes to work, she usually takes a cold shower to <u>wake herself up</u>.

（潔咪在去工作之前，她通常會沖個冷水澡讓頭腦清醒。）

unit 02

Being Slow Makes Things Go Fast.
慢慢來，比較快

片語搶先看

1. right away 立刻	2. so far 到目前為止
3. look up 查出	4. take one's time 按照⋯⋯的步調
5. wait for 等待	6. at last 最後
7. take part in 參與	

看日記學英文

After visiting Mr. Steinfeld, I examined my performance right away by asking questions like this: "Did Mr. Steinfeld and I have a real meaningful conversation? Did I understand his business and even educate him? Was I open-minded and being willing to listen?" Although my answers to those questions seem to be negative, I have been proud of myself for being

Ep 3：A Job, A Career, Or A Calling? ╱ 一份工作、一份職業，還是一個志業？
Unit 02 Being Slow Makes Things Go Fast. ╱ 慢慢來，比較快

1
PART
圖解介系詞篇

2
PART
看故事學片語篇

able to think like a top salesperson so far. I looked up those tips for successful sales reps on Google, though most of which are very abstract for me. But I don't want to rush. I decide to take my time. Being slow makes things go fast. I believe I am on the way of becoming one of them. Mr. Steinfeld is still thinking if the deal I offer is beneficial to him. Then what I can do is to wait for his answer. Later today on my way home, I mapped out an excellent plan that will definitely make the deal succeed at last. I think I am going to take part in Mr. Steinfeld's life. Well, not in romantic way, of course, but in business way because I'm a straight.

　　拜訪完史坦菲德先生後，我立刻問這些問題來檢視自己剛才的表現：「我跟史坦菲德先生的對話是有意義的嗎？我了解他的經營模式進而能夠教育他嗎？我是否心胸開闊並當一個好的聆聽者？」，雖然我對以上問題的答案好像是否定的，但是我對自己能夠像一位頂尖銷售員一樣思考甚感驕傲。我是在谷歌搜尋到這些成功銷售員的技巧，而這些技巧大部分對我來說都太過抽象了，但是我不想急，我想要按照我自己的步調，慢慢來，比較快，我相信我是走在通往成功銷售員之路的。史坦菲德先生目前還在思考這筆交易是否對他有利，既然這樣，我也只能等他的答案了。今天稍晚時，在我回家的路上，我想出一個超棒的計劃一定能拿到這個案子，我想我就快要能成為史坦菲德先生生活的一部分了，當然不是那種愛情生活，我可是個直男，我指的是他的事業。

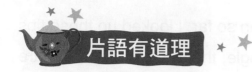

片語有道理

♠ 要表達某件事情到了尾聲、最後、結局,也就是該事情發展的終點時:

使用表達時間的副詞:
finally 最後
eventually 最後
lastly 最後

上述的介系詞片語所表達的語意均為「最後」,基本上可以交互使用,但是在使用情境上有些微的差異:

> 如果你想表達某個事件,是在一件事情的最後一步時,
> 你會使用 *finally*:

❶ The new teacher <u>finally</u> managed to get her students' attention.

(那位新老師終於引起他學生的注意力了。)

❷ <u>Finally</u>, put the sauce on the chicken.

(最後,將醬汁淋在雞露肉上。)

> 如果你要描述某件事情在漫長的等待後終於發生了 **(after a long wait)**，使用 **eventually**：

I believe that the Portland Trail Blazers will win a NBA championship <u>eventually</u>.

（我相信波特蘭的拓荒者隊最終一定會贏得美國職籃總冠軍。）

♠ 要表達某件事情到了尾聲、最後、結局，也就是該事情發展的終點時：

也可以使用表達時間的介系詞片語，扮演副詞的角色：
at last 最後
at long last 最後
in the long run 最後

上述的介系詞片語所表達的語意均為「最後」，基本上可以交換使用，但是在語言的使用上有些微的差異，例如：at long last 會比 at last 更強調「最後的結尾」，at long last 不只表達某件事結尾之意，其中 long 表達了過程之漫長，當你使用 at long last 時會比 at last 更凸顯出「經過漫長的努力，結果終於怎麼樣了」。

- 請比較下列兩句：

❶ Only few companies survive the economic recession <u>at last</u>.

只有很少的公司最後撐過經濟蕭條。

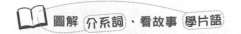

❷ Only few companies survive the economic recession <u>at long last</u>.

只有很少的公司最後撐過漫長的經濟蕭條。

其它

Many couples realized that <u>in the long run</u>, those arguments wouldn't seem to matter that much.

很多夫妻最後才瞭解那些爭吵其實沒有很重要。

> 註 曾經有一位賽跑者（runner）堅持跑到最後，在那個情境下有人就使用 in the long run 來描述該情境。

♠ last 持續、at last 最後

語意（meaning）由語境（context）決定：last 英文意思為 endure（持久）及 go on existing（持續存在著）。last 在古英文中原為 footprint（腳印）及 track（行蹤）之意，引申 following others（遵循他人之腳步），請想像，當你持續遵循某個先人之成功的足跡直到最後之情境：last (v.) 持續、last (n.) 最後。

- 生活應用之開會 Last 遲到的（*adj.*）：

In terms of attending a meeting, Ava <u>is almost always a few</u> <u>minutes late</u>.

只要跟開會扯上關係，艾娃總是會習慣性遲到幾分鐘。

Ava: Sorry I'm late. Again.

（抱歉我又遲到了。）

Viktor: You are the last, and the meeting is over.

（你是最後一個到的，而且會議結束了。）

Ava: No way. I am just ten minutes late.

（亂講，我不過遲到十分鐘。）

Victor: The meeting only lasted for a few minutes. And it turns out that you are going to be the leader of the new project.

（會議只持續了幾分鐘而已，而且會議結果是你將是新案子的負責人。）

Sign A Partnership Agreement
簽約吧！

 片語搶先看

1. place an order 下訂單	2. deliver something to somebody 將某物送至某人
3. turn a deaf ear to 對某事充耳不聞	4. be aware of 當心
5. take something into account 將……納入考量	6. sign a partnership agreement 簽訂合夥人合約

 看對話學英文

Customers usually place their order between May to June so that they can have their new products ready for the new season. It is the busiest season for Mr. Steinfeld and his employees. Seeing that many delivery issues occurred last year, Mr. Steinfeld has decided to change his courier. He is meeting James today.

顧客通常在五月到七月間下訂單，這樣他們就可以在新一季來臨前準備好新品。這個期間是史坦菲德先生與他的員工的忙季。有鑒於去年很多貨物運送的議題，史坦菲德先生決定要換快遞公司。他今天就會跟詹姆士面談。

J ▶ James 詹姆士　　　　**S** ▶ Mr. Steinfeld 史坦菲德先生

J I can tell it's a busy season from the noise of machines.

（從機器的忙碌聲來看，最近是旺季吧？）

S Ho,ho,ho! Winter is coming. Snow is going to cover the surface. People all over the world need to keep their head warm.

（呵哈哈！冬天要來了，雪就要覆蓋大地了，各地的人們都需要帽子來為頭部保暖。）

J I love the snow.

（我喜歡下雪。）

S If you are lucky, you can even see the bright white blanket covering the surface.

（如果你幸運的話，你可以看到如地毯般的雪覆蓋著大地。）

J But we live in a tropical country. We never have drastically cold winters.

（不過我們所住的地屬於熱帶，我們沒有嚴冬的。）

S That's true. So 90% of my customers are from cold areas.

（沒錯，所以我百分之九十的客戶都來自寒冷地區。）

J Then our service connects your customer and you. We deliver packages to your customers' door, no matter where it is.

（所以我們的服務就把你跟客戶連在一起了。我們能把包裹送到客戶的手上，不論地點在哪。）

S I am sorry that I turned a deaf ear to your proposal when I first met you. I have taken everything into account. I'm now pretty aware of the advantages of our future partnership. Shall we sign a partnership agreement today?

（真抱歉第一次見到你時，對你的企劃充耳不聞。我已經做了周全的考量，也了解了我們未來的合作所能帶來的優勢，今天就來簽合約吧？）

J YES! YES! YES! I have been waiting for it for so long.

（好！好！太好了！我等你的首肯等好久了。）

 片語有道理

♠ 表達對某事「屏除在外」的狀況，如：漠不關心、毫不在乎，常見的單詞為：

ignore (v.) 忽視、不理會
dismiss (v.) 解散、不納入考慮

❶ You can <u>ignore</u> my advice, but you will take responsibility for the consequences of your own action.

（你可以忽視我的建議，但你就要為自己的行為承擔後果。）

❷ She walked onto the stage slowly, faking confidence and <u>dismissing</u> the stage fright.

（假裝自信、忽略怯場，她緩緩地走上台。）

turn a deaf ear to something/someone 充耳不聞

When Lara wants something, she prayed to God. She believes God would never <u>turn a deaf ear to her</u>.

（當蘿拉想要什麼的時候，她就向上帝禱告。她相信上帝一定不會忽視她的祈禱。）

turn a blind eye to something/someone 視而不見

The woman <u>turned a blind eye to</u> the leaking toilet.

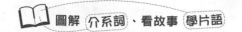

那個女人對廁所的漏水視而不見。

> *give somebody the cold shoulder* 不予理會

Tommy: Is the global warming movement cooling?

（全球暖化的運動冷卻了嗎？）

Lara: Why? The impacts of climate change are still apparent.

（怎麼了嗎？氣候變遷的影響還是很顯著的。）

Tommy: But I noticed that the media is <u>giving the cold shoulder to</u> global warming groups.

（但是我發現媒體不太理會氣候暖化的組織團體。）

 一字多義

♠ place an order 下訂單、put something in order 讓事情井然有序

order (n.) 在商業指「訂單」；在軍隊中指的是「紀律、次序」，應用到生活中，就是「井然有序」。

• place an order 下訂單

Sally <u>placed an order</u> on Fabric.com this morning. Later that day, she contacted the sales representative to make a change to the order.

（莎莉今天早上在衣料康下了訂單。那天稍晚，她聯絡了該公司的業務修改訂單。）

• **put your life in order** 讓生活井然有序

It is satisfying to <u>put your life in order</u>. It actually frees your time for other activities.

（生活過得井然有序是讓人滿足的，生活有條理讓你有其他時間做更多的事情。）

註 get / have / put something in order 讓事情有條理

unit 04

I Really Owe You Big Time
真的太感謝你了！

 片語搶先看

1. sunk in thought 沈思	2. surge up（記憶）浮現
3. flood one's senses 席捲某人的感官	4. face reality 面對現實
5. owe you big time 非常感謝你	

 **看對話學英文**

Mr. Steinfeld is watching the night news as always. Then he hears an anonymous economist forecasting a global recession, which makes him sit on the couch for the whole night, sunk in thought. The memories surged up and flooded his senses. He recalled how he and Tommy started the fashion business, TAO, a leading manufacturer of knitting hat in Taiwan in the 1990s. It all started twenty years ago

when Tad Steinfeld and Tommy were college students.

史坦菲德先生一如往常地看著晚間新聞。接下來他聽到一位不具名的經濟學家預言全球的經濟衰退，這讓他在沙發上陷入了整晚的沈思，記憶湧現、席捲他的思緒。他想起了他跟湯米是如何開始這門時尚產業的，陶奧是 *1990* 年代以來台灣的領導針織帽業，這一切都要追溯到二十年前，當陶德・史坦菲德與湯米還是大學生的時候。

S ▶ Tad Steinfeld 陶德・史坦菲德　　　　**T** ▶ Tommy 湯米

S I have done a lot of research about why people wear hats.

（我做了很多關於為什麼人們要戴帽子的研究。）

T Cool! Tell me all about it.

（酷！都跟我說吧。）

S I believe people wear hats to convey a message. It attracts others' attention, shows their status, and most importantly, makes them look stylish. People also wear hats to protect their heads.

（我相信人們戴帽子是想要傳達一些訊息。戴帽子能吸引別人的注意、表現出他們的地位，最重要的是，讓他們看起來很時尚。人們當然也為了保護頭部而戴帽子。）

T That means every human being needs at least one hat.

（這不就表示每個人都需要至少一頂帽子。）

S Right? Does it sound like a successful business idea?

（對吧？聽起來是不是個能成功的商機？）

🇹 It will be a roaring success.

（一定會大成功的。）

🇸 Yeah, but to face reality. I don't have enough capital.

（是啊，不過得面對現實。我沒有足夠的資金。）

🇹 You know how I trust you and your business plan, so I have decided to be your investor.

（你知道我信任你、也看好你的企劃，所以我決定要成為你的投資者。）

🇸 I really owe you big time.

（我真的太感謝你了。）

片語有道理

♠ 表達感謝的方式:

• 當你收到禮物時,常見表達感謝的說法為:

Thanks.

Thank you.

• 若要強調感謝之意,則可以加上副詞:a lot、very much、so much……等:

Thanks a lot.

♠ 但是當你不想要只是平庸地說聲「謝謝」時,你可以用以下的片語代替:

You are too kind. 你人真好。

Tommy: You are utterly amazing!

（你真的是太神了!）

Tad: You are too kind, my friend.

（你人真好,我的朋友。）

> **I owe you big time.** 我真是欠你太多了。

Husband: I will buy you a beach villa.

（我會買給你一棟沿海的別墅。）

Wife: I owe you big time.

（我真是欠你太多了。）

> **II am much obliged to you.** 我對你有太多虧欠了。

Tad: Many thanks for your support in times of difficulties.

（感謝你在這段困難的期間的支持。）

Tommy: You are always welcome.

（不用謝。）

Tad: I am much obliged to you for everything.

（我真的是虧欠你很多。）

一字多義

♠ flood my senses 席捲我心、lose one's senses 失去理智

sense (n.) 感官，the five senses 則是所謂的用來感受世界變化的五官：視覺（sight）、嗅覺（smell）、聽覺（hearing）、味覺（taste）、觸覺（touch）。除此之

外，senses 也表達理智之意。

- **flood my senses 席捲我心**

  ❶ The strong floral aroma <u>flooded my sense of smell</u>.

  （強烈的花香味席捲我的嗅覺。）

  ❷ You and your words <u>flooded my senses.</u>

  （你跟你的言行將我淹沒。）

  Your sentences left me defenseless

  （你說的話讓我一點防備也沒有。）

  ——出自於漢米爾頓音樂劇（Hamilton Musical）

- **lose one's senses 失去理智**

  ❶ The man completely <u>lost his senses</u>.

  （強烈的花香味席捲我的嗅覺。）

  ❷ The woman <u>lost her senses</u> after she woke up from a nightmare.

  （那個女人從惡夢驚醒後就失去了理智。）

  Your sentences left me defenseless

  （你說的話讓我一點防備也沒有。）

unit
05

Gossip
偷聽八卦

 片語搶先看

1. get rid of 擺脫	2. be supposed to 應該（認為某事應該是那個樣子）
3. overhear somebody doing something 偷聽（到某人在做某事）	4. none of one's business 不干某人的事
5. launch a thousand ships 傾城傾國	

..... 看對話學英文

James goes to the restroom before he leaves TAO. When he is struggling to get rid of his waste at the toilet, he overhears two men gossiping.

詹姆士在離開陶奧之前，去了一趟廁所。當他試著在清理排泄物的時

候，他聽到了兩個男人在講八卦。

⊙ ▶ An old man 老人　　　　**Ⓨ ▶ A young man 年輕人**

⊙ I don't spread gossip.

（我可不散播八卦謠言的。）

Ⓨ Come on! There must be something between Tommy and her.

（少來了！湯米跟她之間一定有什麼。）

⊙ If so, it's supposed to be a secret.

（如果有什麼，也應該是不為人知的。）

Ⓨ But it is not.

（但並不是這個樣子。）

⊙ Does everyone in the office know about that thing between Tommy and Jewel, the interpreter who is fifteen years younger than him?

（辦公室的人都知道湯米跟茱兒的事情嗎？那位小他十五歲的翻譯員？）

Ⓨ Well, it's common for a young employee to get romantically involved with her boss.

（嗯……對一位年輕的員工來說，是很容易跟老闆談起戀愛。）

⊙ It's not as simple as it looks. Jewel has confidential information about this company because she was in every important meeting with him. Although she is young, she has been working for Tommy for ten years. Anyway, their private life is none of your business.

（情況可不像看起來的那麼簡單。茱兒伴他出席每場會議，她擁有這間公司的機密。雖然她年輕，但是她已經為湯米工作十年了。總之，他們的私生活我們別管了。）

Y She does have a body and face that can launch a thousand ships.

（她的確有著傾國傾城的容貌。）

O No doubt that she is beautiful. But there is something more. She works with her difficult boss for ten years. Can you do that?

（她確實很美，但不只這些，她能夠跟難以取悅的老闆相處十年，你能嗎？）

Y Probably not.

（無法吧。）

O She is the valuable asset for this company. She knows ten languages. She is energetic and assertive at work. She tolerates stresses.

（她是這個公司的重要資產。她懂十國語言，工作時充滿活力、有自信，並且能與壓力共存。）

當你想表達「某事件到底該做還是不該做的狀態」時，使用情態助動詞，置於動詞前面，強調說話者的態度：

> · **have to** 必須，意同於 *must*
> · **don't have to** 沒有必要，意同於 *must not*

❶ To enjoy and win this video game, every player <u>has to be</u> patient and creative.

（要能享受並贏得這款遊戲，每位玩家必須要有耐心並富有創造力。）

❷ Principle: Do you really know what is going to be like in twenty years?

（你知道未來二十年後世界會如何嗎？）

Teacher: Not really. So I think we educators <u>have to</u> teach students to think flexibly and work creatively to handle new problems and develop new technologies.

（不確定。所以我認為我們做教育的，要教導孩子如何能夠靈活的思考、有創意的做事，才能處理新的問題、發展新的科技。）

註 當遇到主詞是第三人稱單數時，使用 has to.

> · **be supposed to** 應該是，表達應該做，或是某人期待你做某事
>
> · **be not supposed to** 不應該是

❶ What <u>are we supposed to do</u>?

（那我們該怎麼做？）

❷ As a parent, you are the one who <u>is supposed to</u> support your children, and to be there for them.

（身為父母，你應該是那個支持你的孩子，並且在他身邊的那個人。）

> · **ought to** 應該，表達說話者的建議，但是不一定要被遵守。

❶ Kevin: Maybe you <u>ought to</u> consider leaving Taipei and moving south.

（也許你應該考慮離開台北，搬到南部。）

Gabby: Sounds like a plan.

（聽起來不錯。）

❷ Kevin: I think everybody <u>ought to</u> pay some taxes.

（我覺得大家都應該要繳點稅。）

Gabby: That's a good point.

（說得有道理。）

> 註 ought to 不論主詞為第一、二，或第三人稱時，其型態不變。

一字多義

♠ launch a thousand ships 傾城傾國、launch out 開始新的事物

launch 作為動詞時，表示「將船下水、引發戰爭」之意，也可以指「開始新的事物」。

• launch a thousand ships 傾城傾國

Courtney smiled at him. And that smile could launch a thousand ships.（寇特妮對他投以一抹微笑，一抹傾城傾國的微笑。）

> 註 launch a thousand ships 字面的語意為「數以千計的船在海中」，其實是表達「戰爭的開端」，而在《特洛伊木馬屠城記》中，海倫的美貌即為引發戰爭的原因，後來此片語用來引申為傾城傾國、紅顏禍水般的美貌。

• launch out 開始新的事物，可以指家庭、事業、學業等。

Barbara told us that this is a great time to launch out and do something a little different.（芭芭拉跟我們說現在是個開始做點不一樣的好時機。）

unit 06

Juicy Stories
花邊消息

 片語搶先看

1. pick up the shipment 取件	2. pee oneself 上廁所快忍不住了（口語用法）
3. juicy stories 花邊消息（特別指刺激、有趣、聳動的八卦緋聞等）	4. shut down 關掉、停業
5. stay in one's comfort zone 待在某人的舒適圈	6. get something off the ground 開始某事
7. too many cooks 人多誤事	

 **看對話學英文**

James came to TAO to pick up the shipment this morning. Afterwards, he ran to the same bathroom as the last time because he was going to pee himself! Two men were there gossiping again. James recognized

their voices, and decided to stay in the toilet room for some juicy stories.

詹姆士今早到陶奧公司收貨。之後，他跑到上次去的廁所因為他尿急。兩個男人又再說閒話了。詹姆士記得那個聲音，他決定要待在廁所裡聽聽精彩的故事。

Ⓞ ▶ An old man 老人　　　**Ⓨ** ▶ A young man 年輕人

Ⓨ Have you heard that thing? The boss is shutting down the company!

（你有聽到那件事情嗎？老闆要停業了！）

Ⓞ This isn't news. The two bosses used to get along with each other pretty well. But...

（這又不是新聞。兩個老闆以前相處得很融洽，但是⋯⋯）

Ⓨ Not anymore?

（不再如此了嗎？）

Ⓞ Things changed when Tad found his true love and became married.

（當陶德找到他的真愛，並且成為已婚人士之後，事情就變了。）

Ⓨ Let me guess. One partner is steadfast, comes up with ideas and achieves goals; while the other just wants to stay in his comfort zone.

（我來猜看看。一個夥人堅定地提出想法並且完成目標，而另一個

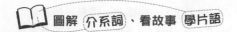

合夥人只想待在他的舒適圈做事。）

O Very close. Then conflicts occur often.

（猜得很接近了。然後衝突就經常發生。）

Y I see what you mean. If one wants to get something off the ground, but the other...

（我懂你的意思，如果我想要讓事情動起來，但是另一個人又……）

O Too many cooks spoil the broth, especially when their ideas collide.

（太多廚師反而煮壞一鍋湯，弄巧成拙啊，特別是當他們想法不一的時候。）

Y So their business partnership is failing over time. What will happen to this company...

（所以隨著時間，他們的夥伴關係要崩解了。這間公司會如何……）

片語有道理

當你想表達「內急、想上廁所」的相關用語：

> **pee** 做動詞時為「尿尿」之意，是較為口語，在朋友、熟人間使用的。

❶ Riley: Can't we go now? I am about to <u>pee myself</u>.

（我們可以走了嗎？我要尿褲子了。）

Danny: Sure. Just one second.

（當然，再等我一下。）

❷ I need to <u>pee</u>.

（我要尿尿。）

> **urinate** 做動詞用時為「排尿」，是較為正式、學術的用法。

Riley desperately wanted to <u>urinate</u>, but her legs ached. So she remained sitting on the sofa.

（萊麗非常想要排尿，但是她的腳很痠，只能繼續待在沙發上。）

> **bladder** 做名詞用時為「膀胱」之意，用來表示想尿尿的狀態，是較為口語的用法。

Riley: When will the meeting be over? My <u>bladder</u> is

bursting.

（會議何時會結束？我的膀胱快炸了。）

Danny: Just go! Don't hold it.

（就去啊！別忍著。）

> 當你在外面，想要借用廁所時，可以使用「bathroom / restroom 廁所」或是「lady's room / man's room 女用／男用廁所」：

❶ May I use your <u>bathroom</u>?

（我可以借用你的廁所嗎？）

❷ I need to go <u>the lady's room</u>.

（我需要去衛生間。）

 一字多義

♠ stay in one's comfort zone 待在舒適圈、in the zone 靈感湧現

- zone 指的是「區域」的意思，而「**in the zone 為正處在做某件事的最好狀態**」，假設你是一位研究生，當你在寫論文時突然想通了，有了靈感，下筆如有神的時候，就可以對別人這麼說：

❶ Don't talk to me. I am <u>in the zone</u>.

（現在別跟我說話，我正有靈感。）

❷ When the writer <u>is not in the zone</u>, he usually doesn't write.

（當那位作家沒有靈感時，他通常不寫作。）

• in the comfort zone 在舒適圈中

❶ Some people encourage others to stay <u>in their comfort zone</u> because it will help them increase productivity and boost happiness.

（有些人會鼓勵別人待在他們的舒適圈中，因為這將會增加他們的生產力，也會讓他們比較快樂。）

❷ Lily lives with her parents. She just wants to situate herself <u>in the comfort zone</u> with the people she loves.

（麗麗跟父母一起住。因為她想要置身於她的舒適圈，跟她所愛的人一起。）

Let's Go Our Own Ways.
各走各的吧！

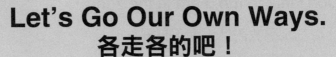

 片語搶先看

1. sip at 啜飲	2. be on the same boat 在同一條船上（比喻兩人都處於較不好的處境）
3. better off 過得比較好	4. grow apart 日漸疏遠
5. partner with 與……合夥	6. leave somebody speechless 讓人震驚到說不出話

 **看對話學英文**

*James is having a cup of coffee at Dream Bean Coffee, located at the first floor of **Excellence Business** Building. The office workers, including employees from TAO, go there a lot during their 8-hour-work time. When James is sipping at his latte, he notices that Tad is*

talking to a man seriously and loudly.

詹姆士正在位於卓越商辦大樓一樓的夢幻豆豆咖啡屋喝咖啡。上班族們，包括陶奧的員工都會在上班時間過來。當詹姆士正在啜飲咖啡的時候，他注意到陶德在大聲、嚴肅地跟一個男人講話。

S ▶ Tad Steinfeld 陶德・史坦菲德　　　　**T** ▶ Tommy 湯米

T I thought we were on the same boat. Apparently things change now.

（我以為我們在同一條船上有難同當。看起來現在情況變了。）

S We will be better off if we go our own ways.

（我們各走各的會比較好。）

T I agreed that we split the company's assets into half.

（我同意把公司的財產分一半。）

S But I would like to continue the business.

（但是我想要繼續經營這個事業。）

T I am thinking the opposite.

（我的想法跟你相反。）

Tad and Tommy look at each other and smile. They know each other too well to pretend that things will work.

陶德與湯米兩人相視而笑，他們太了解彼此了，無法假裝情況會好轉。

S It's sad that we are growing apart. But I will always thank you for your support in our garage-based startup.

（我們日漸疏遠真令人難過。但是我會永遠記得在公司剛開始，用車庫當廠房階段時你的支持。）

T We did make a good team. I was glad to partner with you.

（我們那時真的是好夥伴。我很慶幸能與你合作。）

S It's crap about "don't going in to business with your friends." We trust each other, and we just don't share the same values.

（別人說不要跟你的朋友一起經營事業的話都是胡說。我們信任彼此，只是價值觀不相合罷了。）

Two of them stand up and shake their hands firmly. What James saw leaves him speechless.

兩人站起來，誠懇地握了手。這一切讓詹姆士驚訝地說不出話了。

片語有道理

當你要表達「很震驚、很驚訝腦中一片空白」時，除了使用「I am surprised. 我很驚訝」之外也可以利用其他單字，甚至利用狀聲詞、臉部表情、身體動作來表現：

> 表達驚訝的片語：

❶ He is in shock.

（他很震驚。）

❷ He is in a complete daze.

（他很茫然。）

❸ That came as a shock to him.

（那件事讓他很震驚。）

❹ That left him speechless.

（那件事讓他驚訝的說不出話。）

> 使用口頭禪、發出噪音：

❶ Old man: The CEO's third wife is only eighteen.

（我們的執行長的第三任老婆才 18 歲。）

Young man: <u>Oh my damn!</u>

（真該死！）

❷ Old man: The earthquake caused 200 deaths.

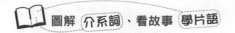

（那個地震導致 200 人死亡。）

❸ Young man: Bloody hell!

（見鬼了！）

解析

Damn 為該死之意；而 bloody hell 為浴血的地獄之意，常用於口語中，為俗稱的髒話，用以表達憤怒、讚嘆等。

用臉部表情來表示震驚：

❶ His jaw drops.

（他下巴掉下來了。）

❷ He raises his eyebrows.

（他挑眉。）

❸ There are wrinkles of surprise appeared on his forehead.

（他的額頭出現了因震驚所引起的皺紋。）

用身體動作來表示震驚：

❶ He dropped the fork.

（他震驚得連叉子都掉了下來。）

❷ His knees locked.

（震驚地走不動了。）

 一字多義

♠ **get the better of** 控制……行為、**be better off** 過得比較好

• **get the better of** 表達「某種情緒太過強烈以至於行為被控制」

May wouldn't let her nerves get the better of her. Not like her sister, May never lives on her nerves.

（梅從不會讓自己的神經質影響她。不像她姊姊，梅不是個整天緊張的人。）

• **get the better of** 表達「佔便宜」，取得別人好的部分之意

Don't let any man get the better of you.

（別讓任何人佔妳的便宜。）

• 在「**be better off** 過得比較好」中的 *better* 為形容詞，表達「較好」的意思，為 *good* 的比較級。

❶ Will they be better off taking their lottery winnings and buying new house?（他們把中樂透的錢買房子會比較好嗎？）

❷ The babe would be better off staying with her grandmother this weekend.（小寶寶這個週末跟奶奶一起會比較好。）

He Is My Role Model.
他是我的榜樣

 片語搶先看 ✦ ✦

1. What make one's jaw drop is... 令人驚訝的是……	2. Seeing is believing. 眼見為憑
3. choose somebody as a role model 將某人視為模範	4. have a keen mind 聰明的、可以舉一反三的
5. see the world through a different lens 用不同的角度看世界	6. open up 開啟…… 的眼界

 **看日記學英文** ✦ ✦

I can't believe what I saw today! I thought the reason why Mr. Steinfield can be the boss is that he is the one who can have everything under control very well. But he cannot, actually. However, he still wants to keep the company. It's

Ep 3 : A Job, A Career, Or A Calling? / 一份工作、一份職業，還是一個志業？
Unit 08 He Is My Role Model. / 他是我的榜樣

1 PART 圖解介系詞篇

2 PART 看故事學片語篇

emotional attachment! What made my jaw drop is the truth that the guy who is dating younger woman is Tommy, the real boss. Seeing is believing. It is a dramatic change, though. I guess Tommy is not as notorious as those guys in toilet described. He is actually a wise old man whom people would choose as a role model. He has a keen understanding of himself and his partner, and thus can make decisions on his own rather than following public opinions. I think I have the wise-man-potential just like Tommy because I get what life and work is all about from the little things in life. That is a sign of having a keen mind. Not everyone can see the world through such a different lens like I do. I think the TAO stories open up a new and valuable way of surviving the workplace for me - to know who you are, what you want, whom you work for, and when to make decisions. I think this will be my quote when the Career magazine interviews me in the future.

　　我不敢相信我今天所看到的！我以為史坦菲德先生就是老闆，是因為他能夠掌控全局，但事實上他還是無法隻手遮天。儘管如此，他還是想要留住這間公司，總是有情感的羈絆！但真的讓我驚訝的是那個跟小他很多歲的女人在一起的人是湯米，也就是真正的老闆！眼見為憑，但這真是戲劇化的轉折。我想湯米並不是像廁所男子所描述的那麼惡名昭彰。他其實是別人會當作楷模的一位有智慧的長者。他非常了解自己以

及他的夥伴，所以他可以做自己的決定而非跟著大眾的思考。我想我也擁有像湯米一樣的智慧潛質，因為我可以從生活大小事看出人生與工作的真理。這就是智者的象徵，並不是每個人都可以這樣用不同的角度看世界的。我想陶奧的故事讓我用嶄新且寶貴的方式，看待職場的生存-要知道你是誰，你想要什麼，為了誰做這些事，以及何時做決定。我想未來《職涯雜誌》採訪時我時，這就是我的座右銘了。

片語有道理

♠ 當你要誇獎別人「聰明、有智慧」的時候，可以使用相關的形容詞。

> 例如：smart 聰明的、wise 有智慧的、a keen mind 聰慧靈敏之人。

❶ You are so smart.

（你可真聰明。）

❷ You have a keen mind.

（你是個聰慧之人。）

❸ That is a wise decision.

（這真是個明確的決定。）

> 其他相關表達「對人之仰慕、讚賞」時：look up to somebody 尊敬、讚賞某人

I looked up to my brother.

（我很讚賞我的哥哥。）

> pay somebody a compliment 讚賞某人

May I pay you a compliment? You are an excellent writer.

（我可以誇獎你嗎？你真的是一位優秀的作家。）

♠ 除了使用片語之外，在誇獎別人時，可以用下列兩種方式來「稱讚」：

> 讚賞他人的策略、做事方式，或是特定的事物

❶ You really found a good way to cook meat! This dish is amazing.

（你真的找到很棒的方法烹調肉！這道菜美味極了。）

❷ You explained the theory in such an interesting way.

（你解釋這個理論的方法好有趣。）

> 讚賞他人付出的努力

You danced beautifully. I can tell you've been practicing.

（你跳舞跳得真美。我可以看出來你一定練習很久。）

 一字多義

♠ See the light 恍然大悟、seeing is believing. 眼見為憑

· **see the light** 表達「看見事情的真相」。引申為領悟、恍然大悟之意。

❶ The accident forced Rowley to <u>see the light</u> in certain things.

（那件意外迫使羅利在某些事情上有所領悟。）

❷ The difference between you and me is that you can't see your own problems. Why can't you <u>see the light</u>?

（我跟你的差別在於你無法看見自己的問題。為何你就是不能有所領悟？）

- **Seeing is believing.** 為英文諺語，表達「百聞不如一見」、「眼見為憑」之意，也就是說看得到的、實體的東西或證據才令人信服。

❶ My brother is a scientist. For him, <u>seeing is believing</u>. Only analysis and logic are reality.

（我哥哥是一位科學家。對他來說，眼見為真，只有邏輯推理與分析才能是事實。）

❷ Have you experienced optical illusions? It challenges the notion of <u>seeing is believing</u>.

（你有經歷過視覺錯覺嗎？這可說是挑戰「眼見為憑」說法的現象。）

The Way to Run Away From Nightmares
逃離惡夢的方法

片語搶先看

1. in need 需求	2. come true 實現
3. take hold of 抓住	4. save one's life 拯救你的生命
5. It's a deal. 一言為定	6. run away 逃跑
7. mix somebody up 把……人搞糊塗了	

看對話學英文

Light House is an orphanage providing care, education, and love for kids in need. The central part of the house is a playground, where kids play and relax. A new girl, Stella, is sitting on the lawn alone, and a 12-year-old boy named Jacob walks toward her.

光明之家是一個提供照顧、教育、與愛的孤兒院，專門照顧有需要的孩

子們。在建築物的中間是一個遊樂場，讓孩子們在那邊玩樂與放鬆。一位新來的的女孩，史黛拉，獨自坐在草坪上，這時一位名叫雅各的男孩朝他走去。

S ▶ Stella 史黛拉　　　**J** ▶ Jacob 雅各

J How was your sleep last night? It's your first day here.

（你第一天來，昨晚睡得好嗎？）

S I had nightmares.

（我做惡夢了。）

J Do you know if you keep having nightmares, they will come true.

（你知道如果你一直做惡夢，夢會成真的。）

S Really? Then how can I stop having bad dreams?

（真的嗎？那你知道怎麼樣才能不做惡夢嗎？）

J We human can't control the dreams, only God can. But I can tell you some tips to sleep safe and sound.

（我們人類無法自己控制做夢，只有神才可以。但是我可以教你睡得安穩的方法。）

S Please tell me about it.

（請你告訴我吧。）

Stella takes hold of his arm, eager to know the answers.

史黛拉抓住他的手，一副很想知道的樣子。

J But you have to promise to offer me help next time. You'd better say yes because my tips will save your life.

（但你得答應我下次要幫我一個忙，你答應是最好，因為我給你的建議真的會拯救你的生命。）

S It's a deal.

（一言為定。）

J So, tonight when you sleep, you will have to keep yourself half awake like dolphins do. This way, you can run away once your nightmare comes true.

（那麼今晚，你必須在睡覺時保持一半腦袋的清醒，就像海豚睡覺那樣，這樣當你的惡夢成真時，你可以立即逃走。）

S But how do I sleep and keep myself half awake at the same time?

（但是要怎麼在睡覺時保持一半的清醒？）

J You have to learn to control your own brain.

（你必須學著自己控制自己意識。）

That night, Jacob's advices mixed Stella up so she has her eyes all open throughout the night.

史黛拉被雅各的建議搞糊塗了，所以那一晚她都沒有闔眼。

片語有道理

抓東西雖然是一個簡單的動作名稱，在英文中，「抓住」這項手部動作也是有不同的態度的，一般的抓住可以用 take hold of，粗魯的抓住可以用 grab，緊緊的抓住則可以用 grasp。

> *take hold of someone or something* 抓住，英文意思為 *to seize a moving object using your hand*，相反詞 *lose hold of someone or something* 則表示鬆手的意思。

The young parents <u>lost hold of their children</u> at the amusement park. How careless they were!

（那對年輕的父母在遊樂園跟孩子們走丟了，他們也太粗心了！）

> *grab* 抓住，以一種粗魯、快速、大刺刺的方式抓住，英文意思為 *to hold somebody or something using all your hand suddenly and roughly*。

❶ On the way to rushing to class, Linda <u>grabs a bite</u> at a fast food restaurant.

（琳達在趕著去上課的途中，在速食店吃了點東西。）

❷ Ira saw a criminal reaching out of a moving car to <u>grab</u> the woman's purse and drive away.

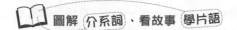

（伊拉看到一個歹徒從車窗中，伸手搶走那位女人的錢包並逃逸。）

> *grasp* 掌握，緊緊的抓住某樣東西，英文意思為 *take hold of of something tightly*。

❶ Whenever I see uncle Ben, he <u>grasps my hands firmly</u>.

（每當我見到班尼叔叔的時候，他總是緊緊握住我的手。）

❷ This is Anya's first time to <u>grasp</u> and pick up objects.

（這是安亞第一次緊握，並拾起物體。）

一字多義

♠ **It's a deal!** 就這麼說定了！、**So deal with it!** 面對吧！

- **It's a deal** 成交。*deal* 單詞解釋為交易，而常見的 *It's a deal* 表達：「就這麼說定了！」也就是在雙方均同意的條件下，達成交易。

  ❶ Anita: Can you sell me your smart phone for half of the original price?

  （你可以用原價一半的售價把手機賣我嗎？）

  Zac: It's a deal.

  （就這樣定了。）

❷ Anita: Good bye, Zac.（再見，柴克。）

Zac: See you.（再見。）

Anita: Let's get together sometimes.（下次再聚吧。）

Zac: Sure. It's a deal.（當然，一定要的。）

> 註 Let's get together sometimes 下次再聚，表達一種含糊的邀約，也就是常聽到的「再約吧！」，通常會在道別的時候用，以表達想再見到對方的意願。

- **deal with someone or something** 處理，特別是指**處理麻煩的事情**，英文意思為 *to take action in order to solve a problem*，常用在遇到一件無法改變的麻煩事，表達「不處理不行」的狀況。

❶ This is the ugly truth, so deal with it!

（這就是醜陋的現實，面對它吧！）

❷ If you choose not to deal with the issue, you may have to take responsibility for the consequences by yourself.

（如果你決定不解決這個問題，你可能要自己承擔後果。）

> 註 deal with 常常後面會接負面的名詞，例如：deal with the issue（處理需要費心的議題）、deal with stress（面對壓力）、deal with the thousands of prisoners in Afghanistan（處理阿富汗成千上萬的俘虜）。

The Boy Just Like You
小小馬可

片語搶先看

1. fit in 融入某社交場合	2. walk around 四處走走
3. get along with 相處融洽	4. be good at 擅長於
5. gather round 聚集於某處	

看對話學英文

Caroline, the President of Light House, is a wise, patient, and compassionate Mama to every kid here. She likes to walk around and visit each classroom to observe kids. Standing outside the classroom, Caroline is watching her students learning mathematics. At the end of the hallway came a tall man, Caroline recognized him, a gifted boy who sat in the same classroom ten years ago. He is Mark Cooper, the CEO of M&S.

對孩子們來說，這位光明之家的院長卡洛琳是一位有智慧、富有同情

心，又有耐心的媽媽。她喜歡到教室走動觀察孩子們。站在教室外的卡洛琳，正在看著孩子們上數學課，走廊的盡頭出現了一位高大的男人，卡洛琳認得他，這位天賦異稟的孩子，十年前也在這間教室上課，他就是馬可庫柏，M＆S集團的總裁。

C ▶ Caroline 卡洛琳　　　**M** ▶ Mark Cooper 馬可

C Look at the little boy with dark hair, Jacob. He shows extreme curiosity towards things and has long attention span just like you when you sat there, observing everything around with eager.

（看看那位黑髮的小男孩，雅各，他對事情充滿極大的好奇心，專注力也很夠，就像你當初坐在那裡時那樣，用你那對渴望學習的眼神看著周邊的事物。）

M I can see that. Also, that boy doesn't seem to fit in the classroom.

（我看得出來，而且那個男孩看起來跟大家格格不入。）

C That's true. I always have to teach him how to get along with his peers.

（沒錯，我總是得教他怎麼跟他的同儕相處。）

M I still remember how I was struggling with making friends, and I still am.

（我記得我以前多難交到朋友，即使現在也是。）

C Well, you have your own way getting alone with people. When you were a kid, you were obsessed with technology and you were always so good at them. Other kids like to gather around you watching how you demo your new gadgets.

（不過，你有自己的一套與人相處的方式。當你還小的時候，你對於科技超著迷的，對那類的產品也很擅長。孩子們總喜歡圍著你，看你怎麼玩那些科技把戲。）

M I still remember the good times we had. It's amazing that we could have so many resources to explore our interest. Thank you for your helping my interest developed.

（我還記得那些美好的時光，真的很神奇我們竟然有那麼多資源可以去探索興趣的可能，謝謝你的培養。）

C You are welcome. Always.

（不客氣。）

片語有道理

人與人間的相處有很多模式，**get along with** 表示「與人相處融洽」，相處融洽才會願意一起打發時間；**hang out** 表示「待在同一空間打發時間」，當你發現你有一群沒事就想混在一起的朋友時，這代表你跟他們興趣相投很融入；**fit in** 表示「融入某個群體」：

> **get along**（**with someone**）與某人相處融洽，英文意思為 **be friendly with one another**，表示與人相處時沒什麼問題、不吵架、平穩相處的狀態。

How do you <u>get along with</u> your parents when you are not their favorite?

（當你不是你父母親最喜歡的孩子時，你怎麼跟他們好好相處？）

> **hang out**（**with someone**）殺時間，在某一個地方打發時間，英文意思為 **to stay in a place for a long time without a purpose**，例如：到你的好姐妹家玩，其實沒做什麼，就是聊聊天看看姐妹的收藏，當然也可以以較負面的態度指沒有目的的鬼混。

❶ The teacher knows where these students would <u>hang out</u> after school.

（那位老師知道這些學生們放學後會去哪鬼混。）

1
PART
圖解介系詞篇

2
PART
看故事學片語篇

❷ If you want to be miserable, then keep <u>hanging out with</u> those mean girls.

（如果你想要繼續背下去，那就繼續跟那些壞女孩鬼混吧。）

> **fit in with someone or something** 適合、融入某社交場合，英文意思為 **A in harmony with B**，**fit** 這個字就是要表達兩件事、兩個人「合不合」的概念，例如人的身材衣服的尺寸、家中的新擺設與舊擺設搭不搭，或是某人在群體中融不融入。

❶ The new wardrobe doesn't <u>fit in with</u> the style of other furniture in the bedroom.

（新的衣櫥和臥室中的其他傢俱樣式很不搭。）

❷ Being an unique individual without hobbies, Andy doesn't <u>fit in with</u> society very well.

（安迪是一個沒有興趣的獨特傢伙，他有點無法融入社會。）

一字多義

♠ **walk around** 隨處走走、**walk away** 離開

· **walk around somewhere** 在某處閒晃，通常指沒有特定的目的地，像是公園、百貨公司等地隨處走走看看一樣。

I saw your brother <u>walking around</u> downtown in his underwear. Is he out of his mind?

（我看到你弟弟在市中心穿著內褲亂晃，他瘋了嗎？）

註 試比較 walk around 與 walk to 的差別：

❶ He <u>walks to</u> the pharmacy at the corner of the street.

（他走到轉角的藥局。）

❷ He is <u>walking around</u> to find an open pharmacy in the neighborhood.

（他在附近繞繞，想找到有營業的藥局。）

解析

walk to 表示說話者心中有明確的目的地，一間在轉角的藥局，而 walk around 表示說話者想去藥局，但是不確定哪裡有，所以在附近晃晃找找。

- **walk away from someone or something** 離開，特別指面對一段感情或一些狀況時，不去解決面對，而選擇逃離。

❶ Jane decided to <u>walk away from her boyfriend</u> because falling in love with him is a huge mistake.

（珍決定要離開她的男友，因為愛上他根本是個錯誤。）

❷ You coward! How can you just <u>walk away from</u> the problem?　（你這個懦夫！怎麼可以這樣拂袖而去？）

unit 03

Secrets Between Us.
噓！要保密！

片語搶先看

1. Bless you! 上帝保佑你！（通常在聽到別人打噴嚏時說）	2. come from 源自
3. go on 發生	4. It'll/You'll be all right. 沒關係
5. let the cat out of the bag 說出秘密	6. Your secret is safe with me. 我會保密的

At Light House. Under a mighty and shady tree in the playground, Jacob is holding a bag of powder and sprinkling the powder on the ground. Sprinkled powder are like feathers ticking Jacob's nose.

在光明之家。遊戲場一棵陰涼的大樹下，雅各手正握著一袋粉末，並將之灑到地上。粉末讓他的鼻子很癢。

J ▶ Jacob 雅各　　　　**M** ▶ Mark Cooper 馬可

Ⓙ Achchoo!

（哈啾！）

Ⓜ Bless you!

（願主保佑你！）

Ⓙ Oh! Hi, Mr. Black, you watch us while we were having class sometimes.

（喔，你是黑暗士，你會在教室外面看我們上課。）

Ⓜ Where does the name come from?

（這名字是哪來的？）

Ⓙ Oh, we call you Mr. Black because you always wear black suit and shoes.

（喔，我們叫你黑暗士是因為你總穿著黑色的西裝跟鞋子。）

Jacob is still fighting his tickling nose.

雅各的鼻子還是很癢。

Ⓜ Is there any secret project going on here?

（這裡是在進行什麼秘密計畫嗎？）

Ⓙ I was just... achchoo! Sorry. That black pepper is really... achchoo! I can't stop sneezing.

（我在……哈啾！抱歉，那個胡椒真的……哈啾！我無法停止打噴嚏。）

Ⓜ You'll be all right.

（你會沒事的。）

Ⓙ Am I dying, Mr. Black?

（我會死嗎，黑暗士？）

Ⓜ Clam down, kid. We human are not that fragile. What's your name?

（冷靜點，孩子。我們人類沒有那麼脆弱。你叫什麼名字？）

Ⓙ I am Jacob. What's yours?

（我是雅各，你呢？）

Ⓜ I am Mark.

（我是馬可。）

Ⓙ Tell you a secret. But you have to promise me that you won't let the cat out of the bag.

（跟你說一個秘密，但是你要答應我不會把秘密說出去。）

A gentle smile appears on Mark's face.

馬可溫柔的笑著。

Ⓜ Your secret is safe with me.

（放心，我會保密。）

片語有道理

在人與人的相處中，總有些事情，你只想讓好友 **A** 知道，但不想讓好友 **B** 知道，這時候你必須交代對方要保密、絕對不能說出去、一定要守口如瓶，英文中也有各種請別人幫你保密的片語：

> ***don't let the cat out of the bag*** 不要把秘密說出來，請保守秘密之意。以前有一個商人要賣豬給顧客，但是商人卻把豬換成較不值錢的貓裝在袋子裡，在這個故事中，打開袋子就象徵著秘密被揭露，後來 *let the cat out of the bag* 就代表 *to reveal something that somebody wants to keep secret*，也就是把秘密說出來的舉動。

Don't trust her. She will definitely <u>let the cat out of the bag</u>.

（別相信她，她一定會把秘密說出來。）

♠ 表達保密、洩露秘密的說法：

tell a secret 說出秘密
give away a secret 說出秘密
keep a secret 保密
You secret is safe with me. 你的秘密在我這很安全。

Jean: What is Mr. Reed's secret?

（李德先生的秘密是什麼？）

Lisa: Listen carefully! I am going to <u>let the cat out of the bag</u>.

（聽仔細了！我要將秘密公諸於世了。）

Mary: Please don't <u>tell the secret</u>!

（請不要講出去。）

Lisa: Nothing can stop me right now.

（現在沒有任何事情可以阻止我了。）

Mary: You once said the <u>secret is safe with you</u>. You promised to <u>keep that a secret</u>!

（你說過你會保密的。你答應過不會說的！）

Lisa: Not anymore.

（不再是了。）

Mary: You liar! How can you <u>giving away the secret</u>?

（你這個騙子！你怎麼可以講出去？）

Jean: What exactly is the secret?

（所以秘密到底是什麼？）

一字多義

♠ go on 發生、go ahead 去做吧、go away 離開

· **go on** 事情的發生，英文意思為 to happen。

What's going on here?

（這裡發生什麼事了？）

- **Go ahead** 就去做吧！英文意思為 *Please do it.* 通常用在說話者鼓勵人做某事，或是說話者允許某人做某事。

  ❶ Go ahead and finish the report.

  （去把報告完成吧。）

  ❷ Eason: Can I touch the China?

  （我可以摸這瓷器嗎？）

  Lily: Go ahead.

  （摸吧。）

  Eason: It's fake.

  （這是假的。）

- **go away** 走開，英文意思為 *to leave a person or a place for a period of time*，表達離開某人或某個地方一段時間之意。

  ❶ Just go away!

  （走開！）

  ❷ A newly married man left his wife a note saying he needed to go away for a while to think about things.

  （一位剛結婚的男人留下一張紙條，跟他太太說他要離開想一些事情。）

unit
04

A Scientific Experiment
科學實驗

 片語搶先看

1. have a keen interest in 對……有極大的興趣	2. in terms of 關於
3. explain something to someone 解釋某事給某人聽	4. figure out 想出
5. keep on something 堅持	6. make good 成功

 看對話學英文

Jacob has a keen interest in the natural world, especially in terms of living things with stems, leaves and roots. Looking for the substance that can be added to soil and make plants grow better has always been Jacob's concern. He is now explaining what the powder is for to Mark so enthusiastically.

雅各對大自然充滿興趣，特別是那些有根莖葉的植物，他很關心什麼物

質加到土壤中可以讓植物長得更好。現在他正在解釋粉末的用處給馬可聽，他的臉充滿著熱情。

J ▶ Jacob 雅各　　　**M** ▶ Mark 馬可

J I am experimenting with the effect of black pepper on the eggplants.

（我正在實驗黑胡椒對茄子的影響。）

M For what? Making dinner?

（做什麼？晚餐嗎？）

J No, it's science. I am using black pepper as fertilizer.

（不是，是科學。我把黑胡椒當作肥料。）

M To grow eggplant?

（用來幫助茄子生長嗎？）

J Yes! I believe the flavor of the eggplant would change if I use it every day.（沒錯！我相信如果我每天使用，茄子的風味會改變。）

M That's a good idea, little biologist.

（這想法不錯，小小生物家。）

J I will be a real biologist in the future.

（我會成為一位真的生物學家的。）

M Why are you so sure about that? Many kids in your age do not have their future pretty figured out.

（你怎麼能這麼確定？很多你這個年紀的孩子，對自己的未來很不確定的。）

J I have been studying plants since I have memory.

（自從我有記憶時我就開始研究植物了。）

M I am impressed. Did Caroline teach you the knowledge in class?

（你真讓我印象深刻。卡洛琳有在課堂教你這些知識嗎？）

J No, she didn't. But she gives me seeds and some books to read.

（沒有，但是她有給我種子還有一些書。）

M Keep on this. I believe you will make good.

（堅持下去，我相信你會成功的。）

片語有道理

表達了解某事，例如事情發生的原因、事情的運作原理，或是事情的定義的片語：

> ***figure out*** 了解、想出辦法，表達想出某事的解決方案。

Seeing her daughter's credit card bill, mom lets out of a yell of shock.

看到女兒的信用卡帳單，母親發出驚呼。

Mom: That's a lot of debt. You should <u>figure out</u> a way to save yourself!

（也太多債了，你自己想辦法吧！）

Daughter: I know you won't leave me alone and let me deal with it by myself.

（我知道你不會不管我的。）

> ***understand*** 了解，可以指了解語言的定義、某人說的話或理論等；
>
> ***comprehend*** 表達理解事實、概念，或原因之意，通常用在否定句中。

Maria: Can you <u>understand</u> the concept of infinity?

（你了解無限的概念嗎？）

Tiffany: It means having no end or limit. It's difficult to fully <u>comprehend</u> it because humans have never really experienced the state of having no end.

（它代表沒有終點沒有極限，但是我無法真的去理解，我從來都沒有體會過無止盡的感覺。）

get 理解，比較不正式的用法，當某人嘗試跟你說笑話或是告訴你某個故事的背景，你不理解時可以說：

She didn't <u>get</u> the joke and found it offensive.

（她不覺得笑話好笑，反而認為有點被冒犯。）

follow 領會，當你聽不懂某人的解說時，可以這麼說：

I can't <u>follow</u> you. Can you slow it down?

（我聽不懂，你可以說慢點嗎？）

一字多義

♠ 成功 make good、好好利用 make good use of、有道理 make sense

- **make good** 成功，英文意思為 *be successfully in something*，表示在某方面很成功。

The young man <u>makes good</u> as a manager.

（那位年輕人當主管當得很成功。）

PART 1 圖解介系詞篇

PART 2 看故事學片語篇

- 好好利用 **make good use of**，英文意思為 *to use something well for ones' purpose*，表示將某事或某物做完善的利用，已達成目的。

Leo: You are so busy after you retired.

（你退休後是如此忙碌。）

May: It's my second life, so I make good use of my time.

（這是我的第二人生，所以我當然要好好利用時間。）

- 有道理 **make sense**，英文意思為 *can be understood,* 表示某事情可以被理解，也就是在某人的認知範圍內是合理的，可以被接受的。

What my boss says doesn't make any sense to me.

（我老闆說的根本不合理。）

Don't Lie To Me.
別耍我！

片語搶先看

1. be made a fool 受騙	2. ten to one 十之八九
3. beside oneself 發狂	4. lie to someone 欺騙
5. for my sins 都是我的錯（英國與澳洲的 表達幽默的用法）	

看對話學英文

With days of trying to sleep and keep half awake but ending up with having sleeping problems, Stella finally realizes that she was made a fool by Jacob ten to one. Stella was all beside herself with anger, and thus went directly to Jacob.

經過幾天嘗試睡覺時讓一半腦袋清醒但是失敗，還弄出睡眠問題後，史黛拉終於發現她十之八九是被雅各騙了。她非常生氣，氣沖沖地去找雅各。

S ▶ Stella 史黛拉　　　**J** ▶ Jacob 雅各

S You are a liar. You lie to me! Why did you do that to me?

（你是個騙子，你騙我！為什麼要這樣對我？）

J I ask myself the same question.

（我也是很疑惑自己為何要這樣。）

S Can't you stop joking?

（可以別再開玩笑了嗎？）

J That's what I would like to know.

（我也想知道答案。）

S That means you were lying.

（所以你就是騙我。）

J Yes, for my sins, I did lie to you.

（是，都是我的錯，我的確騙了妳。）

S And I was such a fool to believe you.

（我竟然傻傻讓你騙。）

J I was just trying to draw your attention and leave a good impression on you.

（我只是想要吸引你的注意力，留下好印象而已。）

S Well, you obviously failed. I hate you now.

（嗯哼，顯然你失敗了，我現在討厭你。）

Before Jacob could apologize, Stella walked away.

在雅各說出抱歉之前，史黛拉就走開了。

J Stella, I am sorry.

（我很抱歉，史黛拉。）

Stella was not responding as if she didn't hear him.

史黛拉沒有回答，好像她沒聽到一樣。

J Can you please forgive me?

（你可以原諒我嗎？）

Stella kept walking without looking back.

史黛拉繼續走著，沒有回頭。

S I would do anything for you only if you forgive me.

（我可以為你做任何事，只要你原諒我。）

Stella turned around and said,

史黛拉轉頭，回答道：

S Okay, then, you are forgiven now. Keep your promise.

（好，那麼你現在被原諒了。你要遵守承諾。）

片語有道理

人有很多種情緒（emotions），以下舉出常見的人類情緒：

正面的情緒	負面的情緒
delighted 高興的 satisfied 滿足的 strong 態度堅決的 relaxed 放鬆的 confident 有自信的	angry 生氣的 dissatisfied 不滿的 hesitant 猶豫不決的 stressed 壓力大的 anxious 焦慮的

英文中的情緒 emotion，英文意思為 the feelings，也就是你的感受、感覺，表達情緒的形容詞有：

emotional 形容詞，情緒激動的，例如：憤怒、想哭等情緒。當你覺得別人，或事後覺得自己沒有必要情緒這麼激動時，就可這麼說：

Sorry for <u>being emotional</u> that evening.

（抱歉我那晚有點激動。）

moody 形容詞，陰晴不定的，壞脾氣的。

Kevin is the least person I want to co-work with because <u>he is so moody</u>.

（凱文是我最不想共事的人，因為他陰晴不定。）

而當情緒已經到了極端、太超過，直逼瘋了的境界的時候，以下介紹形容某人「瘋了」的片語，這邊的瘋了指的是情緒的極端，並不是指精神上的疾病。

beside oneself 瘋了，表達某種情緒太過極端。

I think Larry needs help. He is <u>beside himself</u> with worry and agony.（我覺得賴瑞需要幫助，他已經憂慮痛苦到了瘋了的地步了。）

drive somebody up the wall 把某人逼瘋，也就是惹惱某人的意思。

Can't you stop playing that music repetitively? It's <u>driving me up the wall</u>.（你可以不要再重複播放那個音樂了嗎？我快被你搞瘋了。）

drive somebody nuts 把某人逼瘋，也就是惹惱某人的意思，等同於 *drive somebody up the wall*。

I am a high school boy. My mom <u>is driving me nuts</u>.

（我是個高中的男生，我媽媽快把我逼瘋了。）

註 nuts 原為「堅果」之意，後來被引申為「人的頭」、「某人的頭腦不正常」。

一字多義

♠ ten to one 十之八九、one over the eight 喝醉了

- **ten to one** 十之八九，預測某件事情一定會發生，或不會發生的時候使用：

  ❶ Ten to one this is a trick!

  （這個十之八九是陷阱！）

  ❷ Brother: Anita says the chance of winning the lottery is ten to one.

  （艾妮塔說我們贏得樂透的機率是十之八九。）

  Sister: I don't know why she is so sure about it.

  （我真不懂為何她如此肯定。）

- **one over the eight** 喝醉了，有個傳說，一般的酒徒（*drinker*）可以喝八杯啤酒不醉，而當喝了第九杯時，就醉了。

  She has had one over the eight. I'll take her home.

  （她已經喝醉了，我會帶她回家。）

For Some Reason, She Trusts Him.
就是信任他

片語搶先看

1. look out on 朝向	2. wind through 蜿蜒
3. at stake 有風險	4. for some reason 因為一些一時說不上來的原因
5. stick to 堅持住	6. get even with 報復

看對話學英文

Light House is located in the suburban area. The students' dormitory looks out on the mountain. Beside the building is a long path winding through the woods. Caroline and the students are going hiking this morning.

光明之家位於郊區地帶，而學生的宿舍面向著山林，宿舍的旁邊，是一條蜿蜒的小徑通往樹林。卡洛琳和學生們今天早上要去健行。

S ▶ Stella 史黛拉　**J** ▶ Jacob 雅各　**C** ▶ Caroline 卡洛琳

J Hey, follow me. I'll show you something.

（你跟我來，給你看一個東西。）

S Not interested.

（沒興趣。）

Jacob ignores Stella's refusal and keeps following her step. All of a sudden, one of kids has a heart attack and faints.

雅各不顧史黛拉的拒絕，繼續跟在她後面。突然間有一個孩子心臟病發作，昏倒在地。

J Help!

（救命啊！）

Caroline runs to the kid to check if he needs CPR.

卡洛琳跑過來，並確認這個孩子是否需要做心肺復甦術。

C His life is at stake.

（他現在性命垂危。）

Stella is overwhelmed by the fear of death, and instinctively, she holds Jacob's arm tight. For some reason, she trusts him. Jacob is surprised and feels happy to see Stella putting her little chick on his arm.

史黛拉因為害怕面對死亡而嚇著了,她直覺緊抓住雅各的手臂。不知什
麼原因,她就是相信他。雅各雖然驚訝,但是很開心看著史黛拉將她小
巧的下巴放在他的手臂上。

S Why are you laughing?

（你在笑什麼？）

J Nothing.

（沒什麼。）

S Our friend is dying. How could you!

（我們的朋友正在生死一瞬間,你怎麼可以！）

J Sorry. I am happy because you seem to forgive me about...
you know what.

（抱歉。因為你感覺好像原諒我了,你知道的,所以有點開心。）

S Well, if you don't stick to your promise, I will get even with
you.

（嗯哼,但如果你不遵守你的承諾,我可是不會放過你的。）

 片語有道理

當你答應別人某件事情，並堅持做到、遵守諾言時，可以這麼用：

> ***keep one's promise*** 遵守某人說過的事

❶ Will you <u>keep your promise</u> to look after Dad when I'm not around?

（當我不在的時候你會照顧爸，就像你答應的那樣對吧？）

❷ That man has a hard time <u>keeping his promise</u>. I am his sister, and I know exactly how he always goes back on his promise.

（那個男人無法遵守諾言。我是他的姊姊，我完全了解他是如何總是背棄承諾的。）

當你計畫一件事情，決定要堅持到底時，可以這麼用：

> ***hold oneself to*** 使自己或某人遵守協議

❶ When a single father tries to prove he could be a mother, he should <u>hold himself to</u> a higher standard.

（當一位單親爸爸想證明他可以扮演媽媽的角色時，他應該要對自己要求高一點。）

❷ Will the advocate for national health care <u>hold himself to</u> the same standard that he expects everyone else to?

（當那位全民健保的擁護者對其他人有所要求時，他也會這樣要求自己嗎？）

> *stick to* 堅持某計畫、試著遵循而不背道而馳。

❶ The experienced business man suggested we <u>stick to</u> the magic number, 99, as a pricing strategy.

（那個有經驗的商人建議我們要採用魔法數字，九十九，作為價格策略。）

❷ When striving for excellence, <u>stick to</u> doing what you are good at.

（要追求卓越，要堅持做你擅長的事情。）

一字多義

♠ **an even break** 得到公平的機會、**get even** 報仇

♠ **even** 做形容詞用時，為「公平之意」，也就是「比較」兩者或以上的事件時，得出差不多、一樣的狀態，例如：The two students'grades are even.（這兩位學生的成績差不多）。

· **get an even break** 得到公平競爭的機會，得以伸展志向、理想、計畫等。

❶ The poor man didn't <u>get an even break</u> in the Top Chef Competition.

（那位可憐的男子並沒有在頂尖廚師大賽中，得到公平競爭的機會。）

❷ If Tim <u>has had an even break</u>, he would have won.

（如果提姆那時有公平的競爭機會，他會贏的。）

- **get even 報仇**，表達某人陷害你，你也陷害回去的狀況，也就是以仇報怨。

❶ Penny created a scandal to <u>get even with me</u>.

（佩妮造謠生事是為了要報復我。）

❷ There is only one way to <u>get even with that man</u>. Make people laugh at him.

（只有一個方法可以報復那個男人。讓民眾嘲笑他。）

Grown-Ups Are Complicated.
大人好複雜

片語搶先看

1. perform the classical music 演奏古典樂	2. feel bad for 覺得很糟
3. catch a cold 感冒	4. feel like＋Ving 想要做某事
5. sold out 賣光	

看對話學英文

It's another cloudy and rainy weekend in Zhunan Township. Caroline and the kids are having their filed trip. Visitors are holding umbrellas trying to avoid getting drained by rain. At the center of the square, an orchestra in uniform is performing the classical music. Stella stood still and stared at the orchestra's performance while others are trying to find shelter from the rain.

在竹南小鎮，又是一個陰雨綿綿的週末，卡洛琳與孩子們正在此地校外

教學。遊客開著傘避雨，而在廣場的中心，穿著制服的管弦樂團正在演奏著音樂。當大家都在找避雨處的時候，史黛拉則站在原地盯著樂團看。

S ▶ Stella 史黛拉　　　**J** ▶ Jacob 雅各

C ▶ Caroline 卡洛琳　　**V** ▶ Vendor 小販

C Stella, get inside the building.

（史黛拉，快進來。）

S Mama, it is pouring. Aren't they cold?

（媽媽，雨下好大，他們不冷嗎？）

J I feel bad for them. At the same time, I wondered why these people are so persevering and so united?

（我真為他們感到難過，但我在想為什麼這些人可以如此堅定又團結？）

C These people are united by a shared belief.

（這些人的團結，來自他們共同信仰。）

S I don't understand. If I were them, I would use an umbrella. I don't want to catch a cold.

（我不懂，如果我是他們，我就會撐傘，我可不想要感冒。）

J Stella cutie, how can they play the instrument while holding an umbrella?

（史黛拉你真可愛，撐了傘要怎麼彈奏樂器呢？）

C For them, there is something more important than keeping themselves warm and dry. I guess these people are followers of God, performing art through music for people in a way their God wanted.

（對他們來說，有比讓自己乾燥溫暖更重要的事情。我猜他們都是神的信徒，用神要的方式，將藝術透過音樂呈現。）

S Grown-ups are complicated.

（大人好複雜喔。）

J Hey, do you smell food?

（你有聞到食物的味道嗎？）

S Yes. I feel like eating fried chicken.

（有，我想要吃炸雞了。）

J Can't we get some, Mama?

（媽媽，我們可以買一些嗎？）

C Sure. Excuse me. We would like fried chicken.

（當然。不好意思，我們要來一些炸雞。）

V Sorry. Fried chickens are all sold out. How about some stinky tofu?

（抱歉，炸雞都賣完了，要來點臭豆腐嗎？）

片語有道理

本單元介紹表達「心情」的英文表達法：一、「有開心或難過的情緒」，如 feel＋形容詞，表達「感到……」

> *feel* 為連綴動詞，跟 *be* 動詞屬於同一類，後面加形容詞，表達動作者的「感受」。

表達負面情緒	表達正面情緒
feel sorry 感到抱歉 feel guilty 覺得有罪惡感 feel bad 覺得很糟 feel ashamed 感到慚愧 feel sick 感到身體不適， 或厭煩的	feel alive 感到有活力 feel strong 覺得強壯、或態度堅決的 feel great 覺得很棒 feel secure 覺得安心的 feel safe 覺得安全、無危險的

❶ Cecelia locked every door because it <u>makes her feel secure</u> and under control.

（西西莉雅把每一扇門都關上了，這讓她覺得一切都在掌握中的安心。）

❷ Not being exaggerated, my boss <u>made me feel sick and scared</u>.

（不誇張，我的老闆讓我覺得身心不適而且害怕。）

二、「想要做某事」

> feel like＋名詞／動名詞，表達「想要做某事」。這邊的名詞指的是字典詞類歸為名詞的「一般名詞」，或是由動詞＋Ving 所形成的「動名詞」。

- 「一般名詞」用法

  ❶ Whenever I see my youngest brother growing old, I feel my age.

  （每次看到我小弟長大了，我就覺得老了。）

  ❷ It doesn't feel like Christmas without Dad here.

  （沒有爸爸的聖誕節，就不像聖誕節了。）

- 「動名詞」用法

  ❶ I don't feel like doing laundry right now.

  （我現在不想洗衣服。）

  ❷ This is insane! I feel like throwing up.

  （這太瘋狂了！我覺得我要吐了。）

一字多義

♠ sold out 賣光、sell off 便宜出售

- **sold out** 為形容詞，需搭配連綴動詞使用：

  The flight tickets on Thanksgiving <u>are all sold out</u>.

  （所有感恩節的機票都賣光了。）

- **sell off** 作為與動詞使用，後接「受詞」，表示廉價售出的東西：

  Carter hired a man to manage and eventually <u>sell off</u> Mr. Baker assets.

  （卡特雇用一個人，並且終於便宜售出貝克先生的資產。）

Mistakes Are Forgivable.
沒有不能原諒的錯

 片語搶先看

1. catch up on something 聊聊最近發生的事	2. make some progress 有進度
3. I see what you mean 我懂你的意思	4. the moment 一……就
5. on no account 絕不	6. it was not long before 過了不久就

 **看對話學英文**

Mark and Jacob are catching up on each other's lives at the dining room of Light House.

馬可與雅各正在光明之家的飯廳聊聊彼此最近發生的事。

J ▶ Jacob 雅各　　　　**M** ▶ Mark Cooper 馬可

Ⓜ What's new?

（最近有什麼新鮮事嗎？）

Ⓙ I thinks I am making some progress with a girl I care about a lot.

（我最近跟我在乎的女孩有一點進展了。）

Ⓜ Wow! It seems like somebody finds his angel. Who is she?

（哇！有人似乎找到他的女神了。她是誰？）

Ⓙ I am not going to tell you.

（我可不告訴你。）

Jacob should be in the age of puppy love but he acts like a mature grownup. In the next ten minutes, they begin to share their dreams of a perfect woman.

雅各應該是在孩子們純純的愛的階段，但他卻表現得像個成熟的大人。接下來的幾分鐘，他們開始分享彼此對完美女人的夢想。

Ⓜ I see what you mean. She is that kind of girl you want to protect from the moment you see her.

（我懂你的意思，她是那種第一眼見到，就想保護的女孩。）

Ⓙ And you swear that on no account should you hurt her. Then it was not long before you realized that things were going the opposite of what you intended.

（而你發誓你絕對不會傷害她。但是不久後你卻發現，事情的演變不是你想的那樣。）

Ⓜ That's so true! How old are you exactly?

（沒錯！你到底幾歲啊？）

Ⓙ Age doesn't matter.

（年齡不是問題。）

Ⓜ Agreed. Then, what matters the most to you?

（認同。那麼你最在乎什麼？）

Ⓙ Her happiness.

（她的幸福。）

There is a short pause in the conversation.

他們的對話暫停了一下。

Ⓜ I have made a huge mistake. I was being selfish and broke her heart.

（我犯了一個天大的錯誤。我太自私傷了她的心。）

Ⓙ Someone seems to have issues. But, pal, mistakes are always forgivable.

（看來有人有問題喔。但是兄弟，錯誤總是可以被原諒的。）

Ⓜ Thanks, kid. I will win her back.

（謝啦，小孩，我會把她贏回來的。）

片語有道理

本單元介紹表達「堅決不要」的片語。請比較下列表達「不要回去那個地方」的例句：

較弱 ↓ 較強	I will not go back there! I will never go back there! The last thing I would do is to go back there! Under no circumstances will I go back there!

除了常用的否定詞 *not*、*never* 之外，可以使用下列片語來加強「不要！」的態度：

> **by no means** 絕不是

Your son is <u>by no means</u> a perfect human being.

（你的兒子絕對是個完美的人。）

> **under no circumstances** 在任狀況下都不會做某事；**on no account** 無論如何都不會做某事

Tommy: I quitted my job!

　　　（我辭職了！）

Mom: What? Tell me about it.

　　　（什麼？告訴我怎麼了。）

Tommy: My boss spends all his time following his boss. He

doesn't care about our project.

（我的老闆所有的時間都在密切關注他老闆的一舉一動，他根本就不關心我們的計畫。）

Mom: You should not, <u>on any account</u>, develop your boss's career at the expense of your own.

（你絕對不要因為老闆，而犧牲自己的職涯。）

Tommy: <u>Under no circumstances</u> will I ever go back there.

（我絕對不會再回去了。）

解析

under no circumstances 通常會放在句首，後接的句子要倒裝，以加強語氣。

一字多義

♠ just a moment 等一下、the moment — …… 就

♠ moment 表達「短暫的片刻、時間」英文意思為 a short period of time。

・ **just a moment** 表達等一下。在對話中，別人跟你確認事情時，你可以這麼回，請對方等一下：

<u>Just a moment</u>, please. I'll check.

（等我一下，我來確認。）

或是當你在跟朋友討論事情時，忽然有快遞按門鈴，你可以跟朋友說：

Give me a second. We'll continue our conversation <u>in just a moment</u>.

（等我一下，我們待會再繼續我們的談話。）

- **the moment** 一做某事，就發生另一件事

❶ <u>The moment he closed the door</u>, he realized that he left the key on the desk.

（他一關上門，就發現他把鑰匙留在桌上了。）

解析

表達「一……就」，可以將 the moment 替換成 as soon as，如下句：

❷ <u>As soon as</u> he closed the door, he realized that he left the key on the desk.

（他一關上門，就發現他把鑰匙留在桌上了。）

Leader 048

圖解介系詞、看故事學片語：第一本文法魔法書

作　　者	趙婉君
發 行 人	周瑞德
執行總監	齊心瑀
企劃編輯	饒美君
校　　對	編輯部
插　　圖	高鍾琪
封面構成	高鍾琪

內頁構成	菩薩蠻數位文化有限公司
印　　製	大亞彩色印刷製版股份有限公司
初　　版	2016 年 7 月
定　　價	新台幣 360 元
出　　版	力得文化
電　　話	(02) 2351-2007
傳　　真	(02) 2351-0887
地　　址	100 台北市中正區福州街 1 號 10 樓之 2
E - m a i l	best.books.service@gmail.com
網　　址	www.bestbookstw.com

港澳地區總經銷	泛華發行代理有限公司
地　　　　址	香港新界將軍澳工業邨駿昌街 7 號 2 樓
電　　　　話	(852) 2798-2323
傳　　　　真	(852) 2796-5471

國家圖書館出版品預行編目資料

圖解介系詞、看故事學片語：第一本文法魔法書
/ 趙婉君著. -- 初版. -- 臺北市 ：力得文化,
2016.07
　　面 ；　公分. -- (Leader ；48)
ISBN 978-986-92856-7-4（平裝）

1.英語 2.語法

805.16　　　　　　　　　105010395